The Curse of Castillo Bay Lighthouse

by

Sarah Denning

The Curse of Castillo Bay Lighthouse

COPYRIGHT © 2024 by Sarah Denning

Cover Art by *Teddi Black*

The Wild Rose Press, Inc.
PO Box 708
Adams Basin, NY 14410-0708
Visit us at www.thewildrosepress.com

Publishing History
First Edition, 2025
Trade Paperback ISBN 978-1-5092-6005-8
Digital ISBN 978-1-5092-5990-8

Published in the United States of America

Dedication

For Mason and Brady.
May you always keep the light on.

"Truth is the property of no individual but is the treasure of all men."

—Ralph Waldo Emerson

Prologue

The Storm

The wind whipped waves against the creaking hull of the small rescue boat as it fought through the storm. Splinters flew across the sailor's vision as a flash of lightning briefly illuminated the dark figures in the distance bobbing on the surface of the churning sea. Across the howls of wind and chopping of the murky gray waters, desperate men shouted, "Help me!" and "Save me!" But the sea was relentless. The sea was savage. The sailor knew this. All sea dogs did.

A gloomy glance from the man next to the sailor in the boat told him that they understood each other. Too late to turn back now. The men at sea would stay at sea. The desperate cries of dying men were drowned out by the bellowing wind as the rescue boat abandoned them and turned back to shore. The sailor's ears were ringing. He looked down with tunnel vision at the golden medallion around his neck that glinted under the luminous reflection of the moon peeking through torn clouds and sheets of rain. A powerful, undeniable energy surged through his bones that told him something big was about to happen. Something that would change his life. Forever.

Chapter 1

Field Trip

The shadow of the Castillo Bay lighthouse fell across us as we spilled out of the school bus onto the shore. Pushed together by a cool breeze, we huddled around our teacher, ocean waves rising and falling before us with hushes of whispered secrets from the depths of the sea.

"Now I want everyone on their best behavior," Mrs. Rodriguez announced as we formed a line to enter the keeper's house on the bay. The salty air from the ocean blew her hair across her face, and she tucked it back behind her ear as she shot a meaningful look at Marcos on my right and JC on my left.

"Hey, Ian," Marcos whispered to me. "Was she looking at me or you when she said that?"

JC knocked the brochure out of Marcos's hand. "I bet she heard about how we started that food fight on the sixth-grade field trip last year."

"Don't get me in trouble today." I bent down to pick up the glossy tri-fold brochure. A full color photo of the lighthouse spread across the whole cover. *The Castillo Bay lighthouse has long been a beacon that beckons boats to shore.* Chill bumps rose in waves across my arms as I looked up at the lighthouse towering over us.

"Never." Marcos snatched his brochure back from

me and rolled it up.

A tall, graceful woman with long dark braids and ruby-red lips stepped out of the keeper's house with a stack of pamphlets and shook Mrs. Rodriguez's hand. They exchanged a few words, washed over by the gently rolling waves of the ocean against the rocky beach behind them. A narrow covered hall connected the lighthouse to the keeper's house below, which had been expanded and transformed into a museum and guest center for visitors.

"Good morning, children," the tall woman said. "Welcome to the Castillo Bay keeper's house! My name is Desiree Jones, and I'll be taking you on a tour of the grounds. I see you all looking at the lighthouse tower, so let me tell you before we begin that our tour will be limited to the keeper's house and museum only today."

There was a collective groaning from the kids around me, and I tried to make myself taller to see Miss Jones as she continued talking.

"Don't worry, there's plenty to see inside the keeper's house! Mrs. Rodriguez and I have made a scavenger hunt for you." She began passing out the stack of papers. "And the winners will get a special prize at the end of our tour."

The lighthouse tower seemed to draw me to it, like a boat to the shore. Something about it was so alluring. Seagulls circled above rows of white brick in a narrowing cylinder topped with a black cap, and a few of the birds dropped down to settle on the black railing. From far away, the white brick looked crisp and clean, but up close, I could see the cracks where sand had chipped away at the corners of the bricks. The part of the lighthouse that faced Castillo Bay was more worn away than the back, as if the water that swept in from the Gulf of Mexico had been rushing over the brick to wash away the appearance that it was strong and clean and new.

"Why can't we go in there?" JC said, mirroring my thoughts as he gawked up at the tower too.

"I got to go in once, a few years ago," I said.

"Me too," said Marcos immediately. "I've been in there like a hundred times. But teachers don't take us anymore because it's haunted."

Miss Jones started to speak again, but a man in a suit stepped out. I recognized him by his wide charismatic grin and slicked-back hair.

"Good morning, kids," the mayor shouted across the hum of the breeze. "Here on your school field trip?"

The kids around me all muttered good morning. Miss Jones rolled her eyes.

"Good! I hope you enjoy one of Castillo Bay's finest attractions!" the man said. "It's too bad you won't be able to visit the lighthouse tower! I'd like to let you know that we at the mayor's office are working on a proposal to renovate the lighthouse that will make it safe for all of you kids to go inside."

"Thank you, Mr. Mayor," Miss Jones said flatly. "Now if you'd all follow me—"

"We will tear down all of these old, decrepit structures and replace them with exciting new features, including a gaming arcade center and new restaurants, and a bigger upgraded interactive museum with its own dedicated building and a brand-new movie theater! We will build a new lighthouse that you can climb with hologram docents along your tour and a virtual reality exhibit at the top."

"A game center!" Marcos punched me playfully in

the arm. "That's a field trip I could get excited about!"

"Yeah right, fatty. All you would care about is the restaurant." JC reached around me to poke Marcos's big belly.

Marcos swatted his hand away. "Shut up."

I got squashed between them in the scuffle as they smacked and shoved each other until a warning glance from Mrs. Rodriguez quieted them both.

"Tell your parents to vote for Mayor Juarez so that you can play games and *finally* climb a tower on your next trip to the lighthouse! I'll see you all at the festival this weekend!" Mayor Juarez flashed another grand smile and shook the hands of the kids nearest to him, handing out campaign stickers as he walked past us down the path to the parking lot.

"All right, kids, take a scavenger hunt paper and step inside to the main room," Miss Jones said, resuming the tour with something like a painted-on smile. I took one last look up at the lighthouse tower, feeling a sort of déjà vu as I took my paper and entered the keeper's house.

"Built in the early 1800s, the Castillo Bay lighthouse is one of the oldest lighthouses in Texas. It does serve to guide sailors to shore safely, but as there aren't many rocks in the area, it primarily stood as a symbol for Castillo Bay to guide ships to our port for trade." Miss Jones pointed to a painting on a wall full of pictures. "The tower was built first, and then the keeper's house. While there have been a few renovations, the house you are standing in now has been here since 1853, and the family that cares for the privately owned lighthouse has stayed the same throughout that time." Miss Jones walked over to the gallery wall and pointed to the first in a series of black and white photos. In the picture, a man and his family were standing in front of the keeper's house. "That is my great-great-grandfather," she said proudly. "The care of this lighthouse has been in my family for five generations."

"That's on row two!" JC whispered to me, marking his scavenger hunt paper.

Marcos nudged me. "Let me borrow something to write with."

I nodded and swung my backpack off my shoulder to rummage through crumpled up papers, folders, and an overdue library book to pull out a pencil from the mesh bag at the bottom of the mess.

"If you'll follow me this way," Miss Jones said, "we'll revisit the main room at the end of the tour."

As I shuffled in to follow the class, something caught my eye on the wall past the pictures. There was a display full of those little ships in bottles that people build and a wall of different kinds of knots tied in sections of rope. I broke away from the group and walked over to the wall. The rows of glistening bottles were so beautiful. So cool. I'd started building one of those models with my dad once, but of course, it was unfinished and probably stashed in some box somewhere now. Maybe he kept it in his new apartment. Maybe he threw it away. One of the little boats caught my eye. A blue hull with three white sails rustling against the wind. The wind? I leaned in. The boat in the bottle was moving. Sailing in a stormy sea.

But there was no water.

A shadow passed over the wall and the tiny ship rose up and dipped down over invisible choppy waves. Muffled laughter danced off the curves and corks of the other jars. Something about it straightened my spine and the hair on the back of my neck. What kind of trick was this? Was the museum trying out some of the new interactive exhibits the mayor told us about?

The ship in the bottle hovered off the shelf with nothing to hold it up. Wobbling. Shaking. I reached out, ready to catch the floating glass when a hand on my shoulder made me jump.

"Ian, stay with the group," Mrs. Rodriguez said.

"Sorry, I wanted to look at the ships," I said, electrified by the mysterious ship and the shock of my teacher right behind me.

"They are really neat, aren't they?" She smiled. "But the whole museum is full of neat things, and Miss Jones said she'll give us time to explore at the end of the tour."

"Yes, ma'am," I said, adjusting my backpack and glancing back at the display. I did a double take. Everything was perfectly orderly and ordinary now. None of the ships were out of place. How could that be?

Mrs. Rodriguez looked concerned. "Ian, are you coming?"

"Yes, sorry," I said, stepping away from the display. Did I imagine it? I thought back to the night with all the yelling. When I thought I'd seen the confusing thing through my foggy bedroom window, but my dad told me I was wrong. I couldn't really trust my eyes lately.

I shook it off and followed the rest of the class.

The next part of the tour was a series of restored rooms with velvet ropes across the doors so you could look in, but you couldn't touch anything.

"This is what the house would have looked like in the 1920s," Miss Jones said.

"Do you sleep in one of these rooms?" A kid asked.

Miss Jones laughed. "That's a good question! In the

7

1960s, the Lighthouse Preservation Society turned the keeper's house into a museum and built a new house for the keeper's family, which is just behind the museum. But up until then, all of the keepers and their families lived here. My great-grandfather slept in a bed just like that one. His daughter, my grandmother, would go on to be the next keeper and raise her family here."

I peeked through the door when it was my turn. The room was small, but it had tall ceilings and big cobweb-covered windows that faced the ocean. Beside the single quilt-covered bed was a door with a big iron lock on it. An old wooden desk rose up beneath golden squares from the window. Scattered across it were pencils, stacks of dusty leather books, and a collection of brass sea instruments glinting in the sunlight. I noticed a compass and something in a wooden box that I didn't recognize. A bunch of handwritten papers and sketches in glass frames decorated the wall beside the window.

"What are those?" I asked, pointing to the frames.

"Good eye," Miss Jones responded. "Those are pages from the keeper's journals. They would document the weather and the comings and goings of different ships."

The word "cool" escaped my lips as I stared at the drawings. "I like the page with those symbols on it." I pointed to a framed yellowing paper with a dozen or so symbols listed down the side with English letters spelling words I didn't recognize, like *ata, mosa, mica...*

Miss Jones smiled. "What's your name?"

"Ian," I said, looking back up at her.

"I'm glad you appreciate them, Ian," she said, lowering her voice and raising her eyebrows. "Ready to see some treasure?"

I nodded and followed the tour, peeking into another one of the rooms on the way. Smaller beds surrounded the walls, and there was an old rocking horse with wooden toys spread out on a red rug in front of a small fireplace. A soft but distant giggle brightened the room. Echoing.

I looked for the source of the sound, but there was no one to be found. As we walked by, I could have sworn I saw a painted top spinning and jacks spilling out across the floor. But when I looked back, everything was still. Quiet and still.

Chapter 2

Gold

"Who knows the story of the pirate treasure?" With a twinkle in her eye, Miss Jones addressed the group as we congregated around her in the main room of the museum. The added-on museum was very different from the dusty old keeper's house. It was bright white and hospital-clean, with lights built into the top of every glass display. It seemed so nice and well taken care of. It was hard to imagine anyone would want to tear it down, even for a fancy arcade or interactive holograms.

A dozen hands shot up.

"It's a bunch of treasure from a ship that wrecked!"

"It's gold from South America!"

"It's cursed pirate gold, and the pirate ghosts try to get it back on Halloween!" my friend Marcos shouted.

"Dude, stop. You know that's not true," I hissed at him. I was embarrassed to be next to Marcos when he said this dumb stuff in front of Miss Jones.

"Yes, it is," JC said defensively. "My *tia* said she saw the ghosts last year!"

"She did not."

"I saw them too, their whole ship!" Marcos insisted.

All of the kids were talking excitedly now. Some about the ghost stories, some about the treasure. Miss Jones walked to the center of the room, where a cylindrical case held a large golden medallion on a velvet display surrounded by glass on all sides. It was different from the other displays—lit from the bottom. The medallion itself was mesmerizing, although I couldn't put my finger on why. It was smooth, gold, and round. About the size of the palm of my hand, with black shapes around the outside. The circular center looked like a smiling face with sea-colored gemstones in the middle where the eyes would be. It had a chain fastened to the top, like someone would wear it as a necklace. But I imagined it would be a pretty heavy necklace. I looked up at the large glass skylights in the ceiling and back down at the medallion.

"I hear a lot of you talking about pirates and ghosts," she said with a smirk. "There are many legends that surround the treasure."

"Make sure to mark this on your scavenger hunt!" Mrs. Rodriguez shouted over the class as they crowded around the display. A parade of pencils saluted and marched across papers pressed to books or to the backs of other students.

"This is the Moon Goddess medallion. It was recovered from one of the shipwrecks near our shores a hundred years ago. Nobody knows exactly what happened, but the keeper's journals say that a ship was coming to port when a bad storm appeared out of nowhere. Our rescue boats went out to save the sailors when they got the distress call, but no one survived. What you see around you was recovered from the ship the night of the storm. The purpose of the ship carrying the treasure is still under some debate, but we know that most of the items from that shipwreck were originally from Colombia. For decades, divers have tried to find the wreckage to recover anything else that might have been on the ship, but no one has ever—" Miss Jones's smile faded, and something like a shadow passed over her face. She paused for a moment, and the students all looked around at each other and back to her.

"I'm sorry," she continued. "As I was saying, no one has ever been able to find any sign of the ship or any more of the treasure that was on it."

I looked behind me, past the back of the brightly lit room, to the hallway we had entered through. The hair rose up on the back of my neck, and I had the sudden urge to stand between Miss Jones and the hallway. As if I could protect her from whatever was back there.

"That concludes the formal tour," Miss Jones said. A kind of awkwardness had taken over. Before, she seemed excited and comfortable. Now she sounded rushed and nervous. "Now you can explore! Please don't touch anything. You can visit all of the rooms we have looked at together. I'll be around for questions. Thank you." Miss Jones made her way through the crowd toward the dark hallway.

Mrs. Rodriguez stepped into the empty spot left by Miss Jones. "Class, make sure to complete the scavenger hunt for a prize! When we get back to the classroom tomorrow, we will write a paper about our favorite thing from the keeper's house, so make sure to take notes!"

I turned around to see Miss Jones arguing with someone in the shadows and tried to move closer to hear what they were saying, but Marcos bumped me.

"Hey, look," he said. "The top of this case isn't glued down or anything. It's just like a lid."

"No way," JC said, creeping closer and thumping at the glass.

"Stop," I said, turning my attention to JC and Marcos. "She said not to touch anything!"

"I think Ian *likes* Miss Jones." JC laughed.

"Oooh, I'm gonna tell her!" Marcos said. "Unless you touch that medallion."

"What? No!" I said. "I don't like anybody. I'm not touching anything. I don't wanna get in trouble."

This is why Mom always says not to hang out with these guys, I thought. *They're always giving me a hard time or trying to get me in trouble.* But what was I supposed to do? Once I quit playing football, no one else would hang out with me.

The rest of the class had moved on. Some of the kids were still in the treasure room, pressing their papers up against a wall to write notes from a display card or checking off items on their scavenger hunt.

JC stepped toward the glass. "Come on, no one is looking!"

"No!" I hissed.

"Chicken," Marcos said. "I'll do it." Marcos put his fingers on the glass. I braced myself for an alarm to go off or something, but nothing happened. I stepped back, but JC pushed me forward, and I bumped Marcos who bumped the display. The whole pillar wobbled, and the three of us reached out to catch the glass. I pushed the medallion back gently into the velvet, elbowed my friends away, and carefully closed the lid. Why wasn't this thing protected better?

I looked around in a panic to see if anyone had seen us, but Mrs. Rodriguez was gone and none of the kids were paying attention. Marcos pushed me again and tugged at my bag. JC was cackling like a hyena, nudging me back into Marcos. Miss Jones was marching away from a tall stranger who dragged his grubby hands along the clean glass of a wall display before disappearing into the shadows.

I wheeled on Marcos, pushing him back on his heels with both hands. "That was so dumb! Mrs. Rodriguez would give us detention for a year if we broke that glass!"

Marcos staggered backwards, eyes flashing from laughter to anger.

"And your girlfriend would have been real mad too," JC taunted and laughed.

I turned back toward JC, teeth clenched. "Whatever. You're both stupid. I'm going to finish my paper."

"Yeah, run away, little baby. Run away like your dad did," Marcos teased, pushing at my back and matching JC's laughter.

"What did you say?" I glared at Marcos. Blood boiling. Face getting hot.

Even JC stopped laughing at that.

"N-nothing." Marcos backed up. "My bad."

"He didn't mean it, man," JC said, eying Marcos. "You're right, we were being stupid. Let's go."

I adjusted my backpack and turned away from my friends. I could finish the scavenger hunt without them. I could finish the whole school year without them. But when I looked up, I spotted something that made me forget how mad I was.

Two red-rimmed eyes from the shadows of the dark hallway were staring straight at me.

Chapter 3

Cookies and Crosswords

"I can't believe you touched that pirate treasure!" Marcos had his phone inches from my face, trying to record some verbal proof that I took his dumb dare as we bounced along on the bus ride back to school.

"Just drop it, okay?" I pushed his phone away. It was bad enough that I was swallowing vomit every time the bus hit a bump. I felt anxious, sort of like I was about to go on stage in front of people or take a big test.

JC jumped in. "Stop being such a baby."

"I'm not. I'm just trying to forget that even happened. I don't want to get detention again." I ran my thumb over the commemorative coin Miss Jones had given me for completing the scavenger hunt, which had a picture of the lighthouse on one side and a picture of the medallion on the other, thinking about the scary stare from the shadows.

"Why do you think Miss Jones got so weird? She was so happy and bubbly, and then she just—"

"I knew it. You do like her! Ian with the rizz!" JC made a weird face.

I thought about punching it. "Shut up!" I wadded up a piece of paper from the seat and threw it at him.

He pelted an eraser back at me, and Marcos came to my defense with a pen cap. That started a whole battle of flying gum wrappers, pencil pieces, and random crap from the floorboards of the dirty bus.

JC and Marcus were rolling, and I laughed along with them, feeling the anxiousness fizzle out a little. Marcos hit this poor kid named Dominic in the back of the head with one of my pencils and wouldn't say sorry. Dominic had been my friend before, when my parents weren't divorced and I still played football. But like all the other guys on my football team, he hardly talked to me anymore. I could tell by the way he glared at me when he turned around that he thought it was me who hit him with a pencil.

"Sorry, man," I said, still laughing.

Dominic rolled his eyes and turned around. Luckily, he didn't say anything to any of the teachers, and I made it through the rest of the school day without getting in trouble, which is more than I can say for a lot of school days lately.

When the bell rang, I went to the third-grade hallway to pick up my sister Maribel. We would meet up with our grandad every day after school so he could take us to the bakery where Mom worked. Maribel is one of those kids who has a thousand friends, and all the teachers love her. I stood in the hallway fidgeting with my coin while I waited for her to finish talking to a group of girls about a project they were working on and then had to sit there and smile while they all blushed and giggled at me before running away.

"Hey, Ian, how was your day?" Maribel signed as she met up with me on the other side of the hall. Maribel has something called ANSD, auditory neuropathy spectrum disorder, which affects her hearing. She can hear a lot of things, but she wears a hearing aid with an

FM system to help tune out some of the background noise and she likes to use sign language a lot, especially in loud or busy places. I signed back, telling her about our trip to the lighthouse, but leaving out the parts about the floating boat and the scary man. It can be kind of embarrassing sometimes how people look at us when we are signing, but I've gotten used to it. It never seems to bother Maribel.

When we made it to Grandad's car, he had his glasses pushed down his nose, and he was working on a crossword puzzle. "Hey there, kiddos," he shouted at us. "What's a nine-letter word for *Spanish sea rogue*?"

Maribel tapped her lips with her forefinger. "Buccaneer?"

"Seven, eight, nine…" Grandad penciled in the word. "Perfect, look at that! Well done, Mari!"

Of course, Maribel knew the answer and blurted it out before I could even think about it. She was always like that. Grandad set aside his puzzle, pushed his glasses back up his nose, and pulled out onto the street toward the bakery.

When we got to the Castillo Bay Cookie Palace, there was a glass of milk and a warm chocolate chip cookie waiting on a plate for each of us. There are some good things about having a mom who works at a bakery.

"*Hola, familia.*" Mom stepped out of the back to hug us and thank Grandad like she did every day.

"I'm sorry, kids," Mom said, wiping at her forehead with the back of her arm and leaving a trace of flour across her face. "But we had a big order come in, and I'm going to have to prep some dough for the morning. Between that and everything else I need to do, it'll be another few hours. Can you work on your homework here, and I can take a look at it when we get home later? Ian, help your sister?"

"Okay." I sighed, throwing my backpack down in the seat of the booth. I didn't even have any homework, and now I was going to have to help Maribel with whatever stupid project I heard her friends talking about. There are some bad things about having a mom who works at a bakery, too. She worked late sometimes before, but ever since Dad left it seemed like she worked even more.

Grandad paused. "Well, why don't I stay and have one of those cookies too, and then we can all go bother your *abuela*?"

"Yay!" Maribel cheered. Grandad ruffled Maribel's hair and sat down in the booth next to her, looking up at me.

"Yeah," I said, sliding into the seat across from them and breaking off a piece of my cookie to dunk in the milk. "Sure."

"Thank you so much, Dad. I'll be right back with a cookie for you too." Mom rushed off toward the back again. Grandad looked after her with an expression I didn't understand.

"What's the next question on your crossword puzzle, Grandad?" Maribel scooted in closer.

I rolled my eyes and turned my attention to scanning the familiar bakery where I spent most of my time outside of home and school. Shelves full of old baking tools like a big rolling pin with a framed recipe under it and some old mixers decorated the walls. The bakery had been around for a long time, and there were framed pictures of people and places from over the years, some in color and even some in black and white. There were comfy booths like the ones we sat in and little tables and chairs in the middle. Seated at one of the tables was this couple on a date. The guy was probably in high school, even though I'd never seen him before. He was wearing a vintage letter jacket and had his hair slicked back in a funny way. I couldn't see the girl's face, but she was wearing a big pink skirt that had a fluffy poodle on it and tall socks. They both were giggling and sipping milkshakes, but it seemed like everything they did was in slow motion. It gave me the creeps.

"Earth to Ian," Grandad said.

"What?" I snapped my attention back to my grandfather.

"You ready to head to the house? I'll bet we can talk Abuela into a board game or some Uno." Grandad was standing up, and Maribel was already halfway to the kitchen with our dirty dishes.

"Oh," I said, "sorry. Yeah, let's go."

I reached over to grab my backpack, noticing that it felt a little heavier than usual, but I shrugged and put it on anyway. I looked back at the table where the couple had been, but they were gone. Not even their milkshakes were there. I looked around the bakery, confused.

"Come on, Ian," Maribel shouted.

"Okay, okay, I'm coming." I tried to tell myself it was nothing, but I couldn't shake the thought that something was off about the couple. It seemed like my eyes were playing tricks on me. Again.

****

"Uno!" Abuela called out, laying a blue nine on the table. Grandad huffed and grabbed a few more cards.

"Maribel says you went to the lighthouse today, Ian," Abuela said. My jaw clenched. Of course, Maribel even beat me at telling people about my own day.

"Well, we went to the keeper's house," I said, putting a red four on Grandad's blue one. "They won't let us in the lighthouse."

"It's broken down, isn't it?" Maribel signed after putting a blue draw two on the table. "That's why we can't go in with the school?"

"It isn't broken down! That light hasn't gone out in a hundred years!" Grandad smacked the table.

Abuela gave Grandad a side-eye and grabbed two more cards. "Well, I'll tell you the truth, kids. The lighthouse does need to be updated—there are a few code things the city wants us to do—but I haven't heard anything specific about why the keepers won't let people go up there lately. They used to let tours go all the time, in small groups." Abuela was in the Lighthouse Preservation Society and knew all about the Castillo Bay lighthouse and its history.

That's how I'd been up in the tower before. She would take just the two of us sometimes.

"They get funny about it now and then," Grandad said, studying his cards as he chose which one to lay down. He pulled one up, changed his mind, and set down another one.

"What do you mean?" Maribel asked.

Grandad set his cards face down to free up his hands. "Every few years, they'll just close up the lighthouse to visitors." He signed, "It's the ghosts," and winked at Maribel, picking his cards back up.

"It's been open for a long time, though," Abuela said. "I think the last time they closed it was over a decade ago. I personally think it's silly to close it up right before the festival. The Castillo Bay Lighthouse Festival always draws a lot of visitors, and they'll be disappointed that they can't go up in the tower. But of course, we in the society always get overruled by the keepers if there's a vote. After all, they know more than anyone what is best for the lighthouse." She sighed and then narrowed her eyes playfully at Grandad and spoke while she signed, "There are no ghosts, you silly old man."

"All my friends say there are," I said. "But I know that's dumb."

"What do your friends say?" Maribel asked, laying down a wild card. "Yellow," she said.

"JC always says his aunt saw a whole pirate ship sailing toward the lighthouse and that it just disappeared when the beam of light swept over it, or something like that. He says she thinks the lighthouse calls to ghosts of the sea." The newly familiar chill crept up my spine as I told the story. "But you know, JC is always saying crazy stuff." I set down a yellow card.

Maribel giggled. "JC is so silly."

"Sea people always have ghost stories," Grandad said, tossing out another card. "In my years in the Coast Guard, I heard more tall tales than you could count. Superstitions were right up there with regulations. We always said, 'Try not to get in trouble with the government, but make sure you never get in trouble with the ghosts!' "

"I thought you always said *Semper Paratus*," Maribel countered. "Always ready or something like that?"

Grandad laughed. "Yeah, you're right, smarty pants. We said that too."

Abuela gave Maribel a friendly wink and an elbow. She never did that to me anymore.

21

I pulled the commemorative coin from the keeper's house out of my pocket. "They gave me this cool coin, though, because I finished a scavenger hunt and—"

"What kind of ghost stories did you hear, Grandad?" Maribel interrupted before shouting, "Uno!"

I sat back in my chair and flipped the coin between my knuckles, mad that I didn't get to finish talking about how I'd done something good at school.

"Oh, every kind!" Grandad answered, growing even more animated. "Just weird things we'd experienced during rescues, mostly. Women walking toward you on the waves in a storm, a pair of eyes looking up at you from the depths of the ocean. Old Charlie from the coffee shop loves to regale us with ghost stories from his rescue days. He always tells the one about how he rescued a teenage couple out in the bay here from a little recreation boat that went under about twenty years ago. Charlie says they were giggling and laughing when he brought them aboard his boat as if they didn't even know they were in danger. According to Charlie, they were dressed in old costumes like they were going to a sock hop or somethin'. He handed them life vests and took his eye off 'em for one minute to grab a few blankets, and when he turned back around, they had disappeared. No splash or nothin', just a pair of life vests on the seat. On top of that, our recovery team never could find the boat he described—"

"That's enough, Tom, you're going to scare the children," Abuela said, adding another card to the pile. "Uno!"

"All right, all right." Grandad drew a few cards and set one down.

"What's a sock hop?" I asked, finally playing my

own card. "Uno!"

"It's a kind of dance that kids used to go to in the fifties," Abuela answered. "Can I see your coin, Ian?"

I handed the coin to Abuela. "What do you wear to a sock hop?"

"Well, that's even before our time, but in the movies, it's poodle skirts for the girls and cool leather jackets for the guys," Grandad said, licking his thumb and pretending to slick back his hair.

"Or letterman jackets," Abuela added, studying the coin, "and tall socks, of course!"

I froze. That sounded just like the couple from the bakery.

"Grandad, I think—"

"I win!" Maribel said, laying down her last card. Abuela and Grandad set their cards down and clapped their hands. I threw my card down, but I could have torn it in half. Of course, Maribel won. Like always.

"Great job, Maribel!" they cheered, and Abuela handed my coin back to me. "Who wants hot chocolate?"

"I do! I do!" Maribel followed Abuela into the kitchen.

"Grandad…" I leaned in. "Whatever happened to the couple?"

"Well, no one knows. But I'll tell you that story gets wilder every time old Charlie tells it."

"Do you think they're still around?" I asked, considering whether I should tell him what I'd seen at the bakery as I gathered the cards and sorted them back into the box.

Grandad studied me for a moment before resting his hand on my shoulder. "Oh Ian, don't let it bother you. It's just a silly story an old retired man tells his friends at the coffee shop. Your *abuela* is right, maybe I shouldn't be telling you those stories. Let's go have some hot chocolate, huh?"

Chapter 4

Trouble at School

Grandad's ghost stories from the night before haunted me all the next day. It was all I could think about in my classes, even though it was a Thursday and that's supposed to be my dad's day to pick us up. Maribel and I were supposed to spend the night with him on Thursdays and every other weekend, but we never did because he said his apartment was too small and it wasn't as nice as the house.

Sometimes he would pick us up and take us to dinner or something, though.

I usually spent a lot of the day wondering what we'd do after school on Thursdays and trying to make sure that I didn't mess up my outfit too much or get my shoes dirty. But that day I wasn't worried about my shoes. I was worried about the sock hop couple and the intense staring eyes from the shadows of the keeper's house.

I could tell as soon as I walked into Mrs. Rodriguez's class that it would not be an all fun and games sort of day. All the kids were sitting quietly and rigidly at their desks, and she stood at the front of the room glaring at each student in turn, tapping a red pen against her palm. I slid into my desk as quietly as I could and gently set my backpack by my feet.

"What's going on?" I whispered to Marcos.

"I don't know, but she said we are all going to have a talk," Marcos answered.

"*Shhh*," the kid in front of him shot back.

I ignored them and kept pressing. "Why? What happened?"

Marcos shrugged his shoulders.

My stomach tightened. "Do you think she's mad about the medallion display? Did she see us bump it?"

"Shut up about that," JC whispered. "Don't talk about it. She didn't see us, and she doesn't know."

"It was all you wanted to talk about yesterday. Why are you being weird?" I asked him. "We can just tell her it was an accident—"

"No. Don't—"

"Now that we're all here, it's time to have a conversation about our field trip yesterday," Mrs. Rodriguez began. "Class, I'm so disappointed. Miss Jones and I worked really hard to make that trip fun for you, and I trusted all of you to behave appropriately in the keeper's house. That house has survived hurricanes and decades of all sorts of other disasters. It should have been able to survive your seventh-grade field trip."

All of us shuffled in our seats uncomfortably as we settled into the tone in her voice. I glanced at Marcos, who was gnawing on a pencil, and JC, who looked straight ahead without blinking.

"Miss Jones specifically asked that no one touch anything they didn't have permission to touch." Mrs. Rodriguez's knuckles were white where they held the pen.

My stomach felt like that pen in her hand. Squeezing. *Oh no, she saw us trying to touch the medallion. We're going to be in so much trouble.*

"And last night I got a phone call and was told that an artifact from the treasure room…is missing."

The whole class took in a sharp breath and a babble of questions broke out.

"Missing, like *stolen*?"

"Which artifact, Mrs. Rodriguez?"

"The Moon Goddess medallion. Their most important artifact on display."

"Someone stole the medallion?" Students erupted in another round of surprised questions and exclamations.

"Calm down, class. Calm down." Mrs. Rodriguez paced back and forth at the front of the classroom. "I don't know what you were thinking, whichever of you pulled this prank. I suggested a search of all the students and a severe punishment for anyone found with the stolen item, but Miss Jones doesn't want anyone to get in trouble. She said that she will not press charges if she gets the medallion back before the festival this weekend. That's why I'd like to tell you that if you return it to me today, or to Miss Jones at the lighthouse, there will be no questions asked. I will leave my door unlocked at lunch today, and you can simply set it on my desk."

I was shocked. Some of us were capable of dumb stuff, but I'd never thought any of us would actually *steal* anything. Especially when Miss Jones was so nice. Immediately, I thought of the scary man from the shadows. He had been lurking and creeping around, and he'd clearly upset Miss Jones.

"What happens if no one gives it back?" asked a girl at the front.

"If no one gives it back, we will cancel all school field trips. All of you will be required to write a five-page essay about honesty and integrity for a grade. We will go to alphabetical seating order at lunch."

There were more gasps from the class.

"What I'm offering to you is just a nice gesture. Miss Jones has surveillance videos of the treasure room that she can go through. She is just being extremely kind in that she wants to give you a chance to do the right thing. If the student does not willingly return the treasure that was stolen, and Miss Jones does have to investigate, then whoever is found guilty will go to DAEP, the disciplinary alternative education program, for thirty days."

Yikes, I thought. *None of us would do this. It must have been the man from the shadows. I can't let some creepy stranger ruin all of our field trips.* I decided to tell Mrs. Rodriguez what I saw.

"All right, let's move on. Get out your pencils," Mrs. Rodriguez said as she set piles of print-outs on the table at the front of the room and turned to write on the board.

I reached for my backpack, but JC stopped me, handing me a mechanical pencil from his desk. "Here, use this one."

I shrugged and took the pencil. One of the teacher's aides came in and handed Mrs. Rodriguez a stack of papers. She was younger than most of the teachers and very pretty, and she always wore skirts or jeans with a lot of holes in them so most of the guys in my grade had a crush on her. We all just called her Miss Ashlee. Mrs. Rodriguez thanked her for the papers and then shot an awkward glance at me that made me uncomfortable. Miss Ashlee flipped her hair and left the classroom. When I looked over at Marcos, I could swear I saw him drooling.

"Your research paper should be four paragraphs

long," Mrs. Rodriguez said, handing the papers to a nearby student. "A planning sheet is being passed around, and we'll fill that out today. Your paper should include an introduction, two body paragraphs, and a conclusion. You need to do some research and tell me where your information comes from. I have information fliers from the keeper's house on specific artifacts up here, and I'm posting a link to good sources for research on your classroom page…"

"What are you going to write about?" I asked Marcos.

"I don't know, sharks." Marcos started writing on the planning paper students were passing around the classroom.

"I think it's supposed to be about something we saw at the keeper's house, Marcos." I laughed. "What about you, JC?"

JC didn't answer. He just looked down and started writing.

"I think I'm going to write about the medallion," I said.

JC stopped writing and looked up. "Don't write it about the medallion. There was a whole museum full of stuff. Why would you pick that?"

I was surprised. "Why do you care?"

"I don't care. It's just dumb. Write about the ships in the bottles or something."

I thought about the tiny storm in the little glass bottle and shuddered. "No, I'm going to write about the medallion."

JC's face grew red. "I don't care what you do, but quit talking about it. I'm trying to work." He started back in on his planning paper, breaking a piece of lead from his pencil and brushing it off with the back of his hand.

Trying to work? He's just nervous they'll see us goofing around if they look at the footage, I thought. I decided the best option was to tell Mrs. Rodriguez about the man from the shadows now. I got up from my seat to go talk to her.

"Mrs. Rodriguez." I approached her desk. "I wanted to talk to you about what you said at the start of class."

Mrs. Rodriguez looked up from her laptop at me with her eyebrows raised. "Do you know something about who took the treasure, Ian?" She glanced at JC and Marcos.

"I think I do." I lowered my voice to a whisper. "Yesterday, when Miss Jones was talking, this man showed up behind our class, and he was staring at the treasure from the shadows. I don't know who he is, but he was tall and had a red face and yellow hair."

Mrs. Rodriguez sat back in her chair, looking a little disappointed. "I see."

"He was looking around at the treasure and just seemed really suspicious. I think maybe he took it."

"Thank you, Ian," she said, patting my arm. "I'll let Miss Jones know. Is there anything else?"

"Can I have one of the information papers you talked about?" I asked.

"Of course, they're on the front table." She pointed to a neat row of stacked fliers.

I went over and looked at the different options. There was a flier with a picture of journal pages like the ones I'd seen in the keeper's room, one with pictures of a bunch of different kinds of knots, a paper talking about the kind of lens they used in the lighthouse tower beacon, and a paper with a picture of the medallion. I reached for the medallion paper, but then I thought about how JC said that was a dumb thing to write about.

"Can I take more than one?" I asked Mrs. Rodriguez.

She nodded and continued typing.

I couldn't decide, so I took one of all of them and went back to my desk. I settled in and started reading the flier about "Nautical Knots." *There's a different knot for every maritime need, and a good sailor can whip one up in a pinch...* I wrote my name and the date at the top of the paper, deliberately spelling out the word "Thursday" in front of the date. *Thursday, October 14th.* I went to write "Nautical Knots" at the top of my graphic organizer but hesitated, seeing the paper about the medallion peeking out from beneath the stack. I glanced over at JC, who had his head down, writing furiously. I picked up the stack of papers, shuffled the medallion flier to the front, and sat back in my chair so he couldn't see what I was reading. The flier had a big full-color picture of the medallion we had seen on display, gold with greenish-blue stones. It was large and round, and the middle part was smooth and looked like a smiling face, while the outside was decorated with engraved patterns and shapes. I ran my fingers around the circle, forgetting for a moment that it was just a picture.

The Colombian Moon Goddess Medallion

Recovered among the items from the wreck of the ship *Olivia* in 1922, the Moon Goddess medallion is an artifact of gold jewelry that is believed to have been worn in religious ceremonies during the height of the Muisca civilization. Items recovered from the wreckage point to a possible expedition returning from Colombia, where the Muisca people thrived for centuries until the Spanish conquest of the area in 1537. Texts written about the Muisca indicate that the medallion may have been worn by the Zipa, whose role was similar to a king or pharaoh, especially during religious ceremonies where gold was given to the sun god Sué and his wife, the moon goddess Chía.

Historians who study the shipwreck of the *Olivia* from 1922 believe that those on board were on an expedition to discover El Dorado, the lost city of gold. Legends surrounding El Dorado describe a lake called Guatavita where the Zipa would sail out and throw gold into the water as gifts and sacrifices to the gods, and many explorers sought to recover this gold, which they viewed as priceless treasure. Attempts to drain Lake Guatavita in search of gold caused such a problem that the Colombian government made it illegal to drain the lake in 1965. There are also legends of "fountains of youth" and priceless treasure in the hot springs near Guatavita, between the legendary landmark mountains Fura and Tena. The Moon Goddess medallion is thought to be associated with the fountain of youth and Fura-Tena mythology and was likely found near Lake Guatavita by explorers from the ship in the early 1920s.

I stared at the medallion picture for a little while longer and must have lost track of time because when I looked up, everyone around me was gathering their backpacks to leave the room. It was like I'd been in some sort of trance. I hadn't even heard the bell.

"If you didn't finish your graphic organizer, it's homework!" Mrs. Rodriguez shouted over the bustle of students heading out the door. "And don't forget to return anything that isn't yours from the keeper's house to my desk during lunch—or take it directly to Miss Jones at the museum. Do the right thing, kids!"

I glanced at the clock and counted down the time in my head. About four and a half more hours until Dad would pick us up. I turned to JC to give his pencil back, but he pushed through a couple of other students and left the classroom as quickly as he could. I tucked the pencil into my jacket pocket, readjusted my backpack, and went on to my next class.

Chapter 5

Ice Cream and Sock Hop Ghosts

Dad was late to get us. He said he forgot it was Thursday.

"That's all right, Daddy," Maribel said, laughing and taking his hand as usual.

"How about ice cream on the pier?" Dad asked Maribel, who nodded enthusiastically.

"Shouldn't we have dinner first?" I asked from behind them.

Dad hopped into the driver's seat of his red Corvette, brushing mail and trash from the front seat onto the floorboard. "Nah, you can have dinner at your mom's."

"Dinner at Mom's? We aren't staying with you tonight?" I pulled the handle, flipping the seat forward to crawl into the back so that Maribel could have the front seat. She hopped in and shut the door.

"Come on, kiddo, we've talked about this. I had to start over when your mom kicked me out. Then she got the house in the divorce. The apartment I can afford right now just isn't big enough for all of us. I've been working overtime to make some more money. Y'all can start staying over when I get a bigger place." Dad put the car in gear and cranked up the music, something on the radio station that always played songs about farming or tractors, even though I don't think Dad had ever been on a farm or ridden a tractor in his life.

Dad drew in a whistle when he put the car in park in front of Captain's Cones, the place our family always used to get ice cream together after a fun day of splashing around and making sand castles at the beach. "Look at all those people on the pier. Guess everybody's here for the festival."

Castillo Bay was small, especially compared to Houston or Galveston nearby, but our town always got a lot of visitors in the summer or during times when we had an event like the Castillo Bay Lighthouse Festival. The festival was our yearly event in the fall that celebrated the lighthouse and all things pirate or ocean-related and always coincided with our school's homecoming football game. Friday night, there would be the big game with special stuff happening during halftime, and then on Saturday, there would be a fun festival all day. People from the community set up booths with prizes and games, crafts, or home-baked pies and things like that. There were always food trucks with burgers, crazy sodas, funnel cakes, and caramel apples. People usually took open tours of the keeper's house and the lighthouse tower, but because of what Miss Jones and Abuela had said about the tower, I didn't think they'd let anyone up there this year.

We stepped past a painted parrot on the window of Captain's Cones and under the dinging bell of the glass door. Inside, it was golden and cozy. It smelled like sugar and vanilla. Dad, Mari, and I all ordered the familiar flavors we'd been getting for years at the ice cream shop. A lot of things had completely changed after our family fell apart, but I guess some things stayed the same.

"Are you excited about the festival this weekend?" I asked Dad between bites of Jolly Roger Rocky Road ice cream in a caramel-coated cone.

"You betcha," he said, typing something on his phone before slipping it back into his pocket. "I got a big paycheck to spend at those booths on you kiddos. The boss had our crew to finish up construction on the new office building downtown early so we can be all hands on deck for the lighthouse project."

"Mr. McCraney wants to restore the lighthouse?" I asked, reaching in my pocket to take out the coin Miss Jones gave us and show it to my dad.

"He wants to buy it," Dad said. "The preservation society has been fighting him on it for years, but he's working with Mayor Juarez to come up with a proposal. He wants to buy the lighthouse, completely rework it, and make it a big attraction instead of the rinky-dink operation they've got going now."

I looked over at the lighthouse and the keeper's house museum that sat below it. They looked like calm and quiet fixtures standing strong against the water from the bay that rushed up and drew back, always threatening to wash over it with a wall of water if the wind blew just right.

"I like the lighthouse how it is," I said, flipping the coin between my knuckles. "Yesterday at school we got to—"

"You *think* you like it how it is, but Mr. McCraney is going to make it bigger and better. With an LED light that shines colors instead of the old glass one they have now, and a bunch of new restaurants and gift shops along the pier. McCraney wants to put a big arcade and a movie theater where that little eyesore of a house is. Way better attractions for bringing in tourists and families than that dusty old thing. They'll start doing tours up in the tower again. People will love it."

"It would be cool to do tours in the tower." I tucked the coin back in my pocket. "Maybe we could play games at the arcade when they build it."

"Sure. Sure," Dad said absently. "Y'all ready for the big game tomorrow night? Gotta see if this year's Castillo Bay Pirates wear the jersey as good your old man did when he was the starting quarterback, you know!"

Dad rubbed his knuckles in my hair. I hadn't seen him smile like that in a while.

"Wouldn't miss it!" I said, combing my hair back down with my fingers. "It's gonna be a great weekend." I took another bite from my ice cream, feeling like the late afternoon sun had warmed me right through.

"Tell us the story about how you threw the winning touchdown in overtime again, Dad!" Maribel tugged at his sleeve.

Dad told the familiar story with animated hand gestures, although he didn't use sign language. Maribel laughed and nodded along. I knew there was no way she could hear everything he was saying, not with all the people talking around us on the pier. But Dad never learned how to sign. He always said Maribel could hear just fine. It was one of about a hundred things that he and Mom always used to fight about when they were married.

While Dad was telling his story, I looked around at the people walking on the pier. A few families sat together at outside tables, talking and laughing. Some of them were having ice cream like we were. Farther down by the lighthouse, I could see kids flying kites in the breezy October air between wisps of clouds and a few seagulls. A couple of scuba divers were walking on the beach in full gear—goggles, wetsuits, and oxygen tanks. *That's odd,* I thought, looking around for their boat or a diving flag. They tromped across the beach and walked right through the kite fliers toward the water, but the kids didn't stop what they were doing. They didn't seem to notice a couple of people in scuba gear stomp right through them with their big floppy fins.

Between us and the kite fliers, a lady jogged by with her dog and I watched them for a moment, smiling at the little dog's cute bandana. When I looked back toward the beach, the scuba divers were gone. Were they already submerged? It was almost as if they'd never been there at all. The kids just giggled and pulled their kites across the sky. I squinted at the shore, trying to decide if I was seeing things again.

"So when's your next game, Ian?" Dad asked me.

I looked at him blankly, still confused by what I'd seen. "My game?"

"Your football game, hotshot! I know I missed the last few, but I'm gonna catch the next one."

"Oh…"

"Been practicing? Gonna get that quarterback spot and be an all-star like your dad?"

I hesitated, thought about taking a bite of my ice cream, then decided not to. "I'm not playing this year anymore, Dad."

Red washed over his face. A purple vein pulsed over his furrowed eyebrows. "Not playing football? My son? Quit football? What do you mean? Why didn't anyone tell me?"

I glanced at Maribel for help, but she was kicking her dangling feet forward and back and happily eating her ice cream cone.

"I-I-I don't think football is for me." How could I tell my dad that it was always more his thing than mine? That family football games were more fun than watching mom scramble to get me to all the practices? That it made me feel dumb when all the other kids' dads threw a ball with them or helped them suit up and I had to stand on the side all alone because Dad never showed up when he said he would?

"Not for you? Not for…did your mom talk you into quitting?" My dad sat on the edge of the bench, looking at me like I was an alien or something just as foreign and absurd.

"No. It just wasn't fun anymore. I—"

"Football is a big deal around here, Ian. You could be a star in this town like I was. You could get a scholarship and play in college." Dad's phone dinged. He took it back out of his pocket and started texting. After he'd put the phone back away, Dad sat back against the bench and peered out at the shore without talking.

Maribel seemed to notice something was going on and looked at me questioningly. "I told Dad I'm not playing football," I signed.

Maribel nodded in understanding. "I play soccer with my friends at recess!" she said brightly.

"Well, good for you, princess." Dad smiled broadly and put his arm around my sister. "I bet you're the best one on the field. Your brother could learn a thing or two from you."

Maribel looked up at him, beaming. My cheeks grew as hot as the sun setting across the sand before us.

Why did she have to do stuff like that? Maybe she was trying to help, but she just always made things worse. I got up to walk over to the trash can and throw away the paper wrapper from my ice cream cone. All of a sudden I had a feeling that someone was watching me. I looked around subtly, trying not to act weird. All the families seemed to be involved in their own conversations. Couples holding hands on dates, staring into each other's eyes. I looked behind me at the rows of shops. There were a few people in the windows or sitting outside on benches, but—I stopped cold. Sitting outside one of the shops was the same couple I'd seen at the bakery. The guy with his letterman jacket and the girl in her poodle skirt. I rushed back to our bench where Maribel was finishing up her ice cream cone, and Dad was doing something on his phone.

"Look behind you," I signed to Maribel. She turned to look at the row of shops and looked back at me, confused. "Do you see the girl wearing a skirt with a poodle on it? Like Grandad said?"

Maribel looked behind her again. I watched the couple giggle and take turns sipping out of the same milkshake. An uncomfortable feeling seemed to climb its way up my spine like a kid shimmying up the fire pole on the playground.

Maribel turned back to me and lifted her shoulders slowly. She didn't see it.

"Don't tell Dad," I signed quickly.

"Well, kiddos." Dad tucked his phone back into his pocket. "Time to get you home."

"Okay," I said quickly, stepping back to the bench to grab my backpack. I could feel Dad watching me, so I made every effort not to look back at the couple. The couple that Grandad had described from his friend's ghost story, the ones who were dressed for a sock hop.

"Finish your ice cream, Maribel," Dad said. "I don't want you to bring it in the car."

Maribel nodded and picked up her backpack, too, as we started to make our way past the shops to the parking lot. "I'm done," she said.

"I'll throw it away for you," I offered, taking the bottom half of her cone, melted ice cream dripping onto my fingers. I jogged back over to the garbage can as the two of them made their way to the car. As I dusted off my sticky hands above the trash, I got that feeling again that made me stop. Something was trying to pull me toward the lighthouse tower, so I turned toward it. This time when I looked up, my eyes were met with a cold, hard stare, and the chill down my spine intensified.

The man from the shadows was back, lurking with hunched shoulders under swirling seagulls by the lighthouse tower. His mouth was set in a thin, hard line, his eyes intense, and he pulled his big meaty hand from his pocket and raised it in the air between us. He was pointing right at me.

Chapter 6

The Myth of the Moon Goddess

Mom asked us to go to our rooms when Dad dropped us off. Through the door, I could hear them arguing again as I threw my stuff on the bed and went over to my desk to open up my laptop. Something about football, and the house, and about how Dad had to work this weekend.

"The kids have been talking about going to the festival with you for weeks! The games. Cotton candy. All their friends will be there. They expect you to take them. You told them you would!"

"Plans changed. You take them."

I wondered when his plans changed. Did Mom make him mad? Did he decide not to take me because he was disappointed that I quit football?

"It's your weekend, Blake! You know I have to work the bakery booth at the festival."

"I have to work too. Figure it out."

Their voices got a little louder when Maribel opened my bedroom door and let herself in.

"There's no way McCraney has y'all working on the festival weekend. What's really going on?"

"So you're calling me a liar?!"

"Whatcha doin'?" Maribel said, plopping down on the bed next to my backpack.

"Maribel, you're supposed to be in your room. I have homework." I turned to my laptop and opened up our classroom page to click on the links for our paper on the lighthouse.

"What are Mom and Dad fighting about?" Maribel asked. "I can't really hear them."

"Who cares, Mari? Mom and Dad are always fighting. I think that's the only way they know how to talk to each other these days. Don't you have a project you're supposed to be working on?"

Maribel was straining to hear the conversation.

"...shouldn't be more important than your own kids!" Mom was shouting.

She's not going to let this go, I thought. I sighed and went over to sit by my sister and put my arm around her. "Mom and Dad are talking about this weekend. Dad's working and so is Mom, so there's no one to take us to the festival."

"But Dad said he would take us." Maribel's shoulders slumped beneath my arm. "I bet it's my fault. It's too hard to take me loud places without Mom."

"It isn't your fault. He just had something come up. He told us he's been trying to work overtime. Maybe he's making more money so we can stay with him every now and then."

"I guess. I just really wanted to go to the festival."

"Don't worry," I said. "We'll figure it out. I'll probably go with JC and Marcos, I guess. I bet Mom will ask Abuela and Grandad to take you, or maybe you can go with one of your friends."

"Can't I go with you?" Her big eyes glistened and sparkled like the kittens from cartoons.

"I don't know. I've got stuff I wanna do that you

won't like, and my friends are kinda weird about hanging out with little kids." I tried to pretend I didn't see hurt flash across her eyes. Sometimes I had a hard time being nice to Maribel after we'd been hanging out with Dad. It felt like she kept him from liking me as much as he used to. From liking *us* as much as he used to. *It isn't her fault.* I softened my voice and tried again. "We'll figure it out, okay?"

The front door slammed, rattling the walls. I peeked out the window. Dad threw himself into the red car and screeched off down the street away from our house toward the new place he was living. The corners of my eyes were stinging. I gritted my teeth. It shouldn't feel weird to see Dad leave. He hadn't lived in our house for a while now. It shouldn't hurt anymore. I'd watched Dad storm out to the curb from my window so many times that I'd lost count.

Like the night last year before the divorce when I'd looked out and seen—

"Hey, *niños*." Mom poked her head in, wearing a fake smile that didn't hide how tired she looked. "You guys have fun with your dad?"

"I guess." I let the curtain fall back over the window.

Mom walked over to sit on my bed beside Maribel. "So guys, the plans for this weekend changed—"

"We heard," I said.

"I'm sorry about that." Mom's eyes darted to Mari. "I didn't mean for you kids to have to listen to all that. Your dad really wanted to take you, but he has to work. I tried to get someone else to cover the bakery booth for me, but no one is available, so I have to work too."

"So, we all miss the festival, then?" I asked, my voice flat.

"Not necessarily. I promise we will figure something out, okay?"

I shrugged. Mari nodded. The only sound in the room was my ceiling fan humming.

Mom rubbed at her neck. "You guys hungry?"

"Not really," I said. "We went to Captain's Cones."

"Oh." Mom forced another weak smile. "Dinner's not as fun as ice cream, is it? What do you say we just skip dinner, then? We could have some popcorn instead. Watch a movie?"

"Can I pick the movie?" Maribel asked.

"Sure, cupcake." Mom sat up a little straighter, beaming at Maribel and looking over at me hopefully.

"I've got homework." My answer shot out sharper than I meant it to.

"Do you need help?" she asked.

"No. I just want everyone to leave me alone."

Mom studied me for a moment before patting Maribel's leg. "Well, it looks like it's just you and me then, Mari. Let's go get that popcorn started! Ian, you can join us any time if you finish your homework. Or if you just want to."

Maribel trotted after Mom and out of my room. Even though I felt a little guilty for being short with my mom, I was glad to finally have my room to myself again. I needed some space. I needed a distraction.

On my open laptop, I scrolled through the links Mrs. Rodriguez posted for us and settled on one called "Moon Goddess Medallion." A full-color picture of the medallion filled the screen, and I leaned in, mesmerized by it again for a moment. I scrolled down and chose "Origin and History."

Many expeditions in search of the famed "city of

gold" led explorers to Lake Guatavita in the jungles of present-day Colombia, where early Muisca people are said to have sacrificed gold to the gods by throwing it in the lake.

There were several black and white photos of guys in adventurer-looking outfits posing for group photos in front of a jungle and a few close-up pictures of statues and jewelry. I kept reading.

Many of these journeys ended in unexplained tragedy, such as the expedition in the early 1920s where everyone died in a shipwreck off the coast of Castillo Bay in Texas.

There was another image of an old ship with a man in a captain's hat leaning against the hull. The caption below it said, "Captain Ellis Larsen and his crew set sail on the ship *Olivia* and were never seen again." Below that, I clicked on a link called "Gold, Immortality, and the Myth of Tena and Fura."

A illustration came up of a big lake, probably Lake Guatavita, with two tall mountains on either side. A man and a woman dressed in gold and white with crowns stood next to each other, holding hands but looking away from one another. The woman wore a necklace that looked like it might be the medallion. A blond man wearing a conquistador outfit stood behind the trees on the woman's side. He reminded me of the man I'd seen in the keeper's house and again on the pier. The man from the shadows. I scrolled down to read the story beneath the Lake Guatavita drawing.

The Legend of Fura and Tena,
the Immortal Lovers
In the beginning of time, the sun god, Sué,

and his wife, Chía, the moon goddess, saw fit to bless the earth with two immortals formed out of gold to become the father and mother of all Muisca people. They were the strong and brave Tena and the beautiful, compassionate Fura. Fura and Tena were blessed to live in harmony with no fear of death as long as they were honest, loyal, and true. To honor his promise, Sué gifted Fura with a gold medallion of his likeness to be worn around her neck.

And so, for many years, they lived in the lush lands of Sué and Chía between the mountains Sué formed for them among the hot springs and under the green fruitful trees. But their harmony would not last forever.

Centuries went by before pale bearded men from other shores came to the lands of the Muisca looking for gold and immortality. One such man, Zirba, stumbled across the beautiful Fura and they fell in love, deceiving Sué and Tena.

When Tena discovered the affair, he killed Zirba in his rage and vowed never to speak to Fura again. Sué took note of this disharmony and stripped both Tena and Fura of their immortality. Despite Fura's pleading, Tena would not forgive her. Every tear she cried in her agony became an emerald in the deep lake of Guatavita. Every sigh became a butterfly upon its shores. Sué was furious, and his punishments were many. He took from Fura the ability to be heard, and her many cries of apologies never fell on Tena's ears. Tena remained inconsolably angry.

Soon the pale bearded men were

everywhere, scouring the hills and exploiting the Muisca people. Tena killed each of the invaders, each more brutally than the last until they overcame him, tore him apart, and threw him into Lake Guatavita. As he sank to the bottom of the lake, his bones became gold again, and still they rest amongst the emerald tears of Fura.

But Chía, the moon goddess and wife of Sué, heard Fura's cries and took pity on her. She sent a moonbeam for Fura's soul to travel to the afterlife, and as her soul left her body, she cried two final emerald tears, which became eyes of sadness in the golden medallion that was left behind. Chía charged her son, Zipa, with carefully taking the medallion back to her temple in the city where he watched over it all of his days, and every year on the festival of the sun, Zipa would sail out to Lake Guatavita to deposit gold in worship of his father, Sué, and to appease the restless bones of Tena.

It is said that Chía and Fura still usher remorseful and unheard souls to the afterlife on the moonbeam that Chía sent for Fura every common year in the lunar month of Mica, and as long as the golden medallion of Fura remains in the light of Chía's moonbeam, restless souls will always be able to find their way home.

I scrolled back up to zoom in on the picture of Fura's necklace. The eyes. The markings. Mom and Maribel's giggling in the kitchen pulled me away from the screen. *This is dumb. I'm missing out on the fun.* I decided to finish filling out my planning page and then I'd go join them.

I went to my bed and unzipped my backpack to get out the papers I'd hastily shoved into it at the end of Mrs. Rodriguez's class: the fliers and the graphic organizer. They were nowhere to be found. I grunted. Frustrated. Mom was always on me about cleaning up my backpack and keeping my papers in the right folders. *Maybe she's right,* I thought as I peeled an empty juice packet off my overdue library book. *But I'll never tell her that.* I set the book and trash on the bed beside my bag when a shimmer caught my eye. Something odd was glinting beneath the notebooks, broken box of colored pencils, and crumpled-up papers.

I paused for a moment, then turned my backpack upside down to shake everything out. The shiny mystery object tumbled onto my bed with a loud thump and a fluttering of schoolwork settling around it. I took a step backward and blinked several times to make sure my eyes weren't playing tricks on me again. It was the last thing I ever expected to see.

Sitting on my bed, surrounded by torn and wrinkled papers, wrappers, the old juice packet, and broken colored pencils, glistening gold, was the missing Moon Goddess medallion.

Chapter 7

The Plan

"Please, Mom," I begged. "My head hurts, and I feel like I'm going to throw up." I had hardly slept at all. My mind was full of the strange things I'd seen, the icy glare of the man from the shadows, and a terrible fear of what would happen to me if I was found with the stolen medallion. In the dark early hours of the morning, I'd imagined everything from in-school suspension to the death penalty. I didn't know what to do, and I couldn't think of anyone who could help me.

Mom brushed the hair from my face and felt my forehead. "You're fine, Ian. You've got to go to school."

I swung my backpack over my shoulder, the weight of the medallion punching me in the back. "I hate school. Everyone is just gonna be talking about stupid homecoming weekend all day."

"I'm sorry, honey. I'll talk to Grandad and Abuela and make sure you kids are able to have a good time, okay? I promise."

My eyes rolled beneath the kiss Mom planted on my forehead. "Okay," I murmured as she ushered us out the door to the car. "I hate promises," I grunted under my breath.

In class, Mrs. Rodriguez informed us that Miss Jones would be checking the video footage since no one had turned in the missing medallion. Cold sweat prickled my body. *She will know that I have it. Miss Jones will see that we were goofing around by the display and that the stolen treasure is in my backpack.*

When I pulled out my graphic organizer, looking at the word "medallion" all over it made me nauseous. This was the worst thing I ever could have imagined. I would be in the biggest trouble of my life. Worse than the time that me, JC, and Marcos had a food fight on the field trip last year and got in-school suspension for two days. Worse than the time Mom saw me teach Mari how to sign a bad word that JC taught me, and I lost my phone for a week. Even worse than the time I left the door open, when a skunk got in the house and sprayed all the furniture, and I got grounded until we didn't have to leave the windows open anymore. But I knew I did those things. I didn't do this. I would never steal anything from the museum on purpose. *How did the necklace get in there?*

Next to me, JC's leg was bouncing. *He was so irritated with me yesterday when I said I would write my paper about the medallion. He didn't want me to reach into my bag for the pencil after Mrs. Rodriguez made that announcement.* I thought about how he and Marcos had teased me and pushed me. I was so busy looking at the man in the shadows I could have missed it if they slipped the treasure in my backpack. *They would do something stupid like that.* I thought about all the times they'd gotten me in trouble before. I looked to my left where Marcos was happily absorbed in doodling a shark biting someone in half at the top of his paper. I looked to my right at JC who was doing nothing at all except for staring straight ahead. But he wasn't doing nothing, I decided. He was avoiding me.

Anger surged up from my chest to the tops of my ears, blinding me a little. I couldn't hear anything except my own heart beating in my ears. It was all I could do to quietly sit between those two without bursting. I broke two pencils when I was writing from the pressure I put on the paper. Finally, when the bell rang and JC got up to rush toward the door again, I grabbed his arm and pulled him back.

"We need to talk," I growled.

JC's face went pale, and I could tell he knew exactly why. He shot a look at Marcos whose carefree expression was immediately replaced by one of panic.

"Ian," Mrs. Rodriguez called out, causing all three of us to freeze in fear. "Come here for a minute, please."

I shot a look back at my friends, who wore the panic on their face that was swirling in the pit of my stomach.

Reluctantly I walked up to Mrs. Rodriguez's desk, every step measured and mechanical.

Don't look guilty. Don't look guilty.

"Yes, ma'am." I stopped in front of Mrs. Rodriguez and looked at her blankly, using every ounce of my control to keep my face from showing the guilt and fear that was pulsing behind my eyeballs.

"I wanted to let you know that I told Miss Jones about the man in the shadows that you mentioned yesterday. I'll admit, I didn't see him—but Miss Jones said that he's a regular patron of the keeper's house and that there's nothing to worry about. She said she will reach out to contact you if she has any more questions."

"Oh…okay…" I shifted uncomfortably from one foot to the other. "Is that…is that all?"

"Yes," she said, stopping to study me for a moment.

"Ian, I know you've been through a lot this year, with…well, with your parents. If you ever need someone to talk to—"

"I need to get to my next class." I cut her off without meaning to.

"Right. Of course." Mrs. Rodriguez sat back down at her desk. "Enjoy homecoming weekend," she said, smiling.

"You too…thanks…" I backed away awkwardly and bolted out of the classroom as quickly as I could.

Marcos and JC were whispering in the hallway. I dragged them into the bathroom by their backpacks.

"What did you do yesterday?"

JC and Marcos exchanged glances and then stared at a squeaky little sixth grader who was just trying to wash his hands. The sixth grader turned off the faucet and pulled a paper towel from the dispenser, drying his hands slowly. JC leaned back and looked under the stalls to see if anyone else was in the bathroom and gave a nod to Marcos and me.

The kid tossed his paper towel in the trash can and reached for another one.

"Get lost!" Marcos shouted.

The kid jumped a little and scuttled out of the bathroom.

"Listen, we were just messing around," JC said in a low voice. "I was mad at you for calling me stupid, so I—"

"You were a jerk to both of us," Marcos interrupted.

I gritted my teeth. "What did you do?"

"I threw the necklace thing in your backpack," JC confessed.

"Why would you do that?" I balled up my fists and

took a step forward. I could take them. Both of them. I could shove both their stupid faces right into the dirty ceramic sinks.

"Calm down, it was just a joke!" JC put both hands up.

Dominic walked in. "Hey, guys." He examined each of us and settled on me. "You all good?"

"Shut up, Dominic," Marcos answered.

"You shut up, Marcos," I bit back. "Yeah, we're all good. Thank you, Dom."

Dominic nodded and shuffled past us to the stalls.

"You're the worst friends in the history of friends," I said to both of them.

The bell rang.

"Great. Now we're late for class," Marcos grumbled.

"If you don't help me fix this, then you'll have a lot more to worry about than being tardy. I'm not getting in trouble for this by myself."

"It was never supposed to be this big a deal. We were going to tell you but then we couldn't because Marcos said that dumb thing about your dad and…we'll help you."

Marcos rolled his eyes.

"Y'all are going to the homecoming game tonight, right?" I asked.

"Duh." Marcos slammed a locker as we walked from the bathroom toward our science class.

"So let's sneak away early and bring the medallion back to the keeper's house. Everybody will be so busy cheering on the Castillo Bay Pirates under the Friday night lights, that no one will notice we are gone."

"I'm not missing the game for that!" Marcos said.

"Just put it on Mrs. Rodriguez's desk today like she said."

"No way! I'll get caught!"

"No, he's right," JC agreed. "Mrs. Rodriguez already suspects us. We can't go back in there. Miss Jones doesn't know who we are."

"Besides, she told us that Miss Jones wouldn't ask any questions if the necklace turned up. It doesn't matter where or how." We stood outside our science class door, and I knocked. "So we will meet up tonight at the game and get rid of this thing for good. Like it never happened."

"Fine," Marcos agreed.

Maybe we could avoid getting in trouble after all.

****

"Good news, kids!" Mom said cheerfully as she plopped down next to me in the booth at the bakery. "We're closing up early so everyone can go to the big game tonight! Let's get out of here and head home. I wanna get in my pj's and hang out all night with my two favorite people." Mom put her arm around me and kissed the top of my head.

"We're not going to the game? Why? We go every year!" I panicked. My whole plan was counting on the fact that I could slip away unnoticed during the football game.

"I'd rather skip it this year, honey." Mom seemed uncomfortable all of a sudden. "Anyway, I didn't think you cared that much about football these days."

"I told JC and Marcos I'd go to the game with them," I lied, hoping the urgency in my voice didn't make me sound as desperate as I felt.

Mom's lips pressed together in a thin line. "Those

boys aren't my favorite, Ian. I don't think they treat you very well, and they don't always make the best choices...Let's get some pizza and play some board games, maybe watch that movie?"

"I love pizza!" Maribel piped in. "I'll watch a movie with you, Mom!"

Mom's smile returned, and she squeezed Maribel's hand across the table and turned to me. She looked so hopeful it crushed me to hurt her feelings again. But wouldn't Mom be even more disappointed if she found out her son was a thief and a liar? Mom was always talking about "character" and how important it was to be honest. Funny, for me to look honest to my mom I'd have to lie.

"I just really want to go to the game with my friends. I told them I'd be there." I hesitated. "I don't wanna go back on my word."

Mom's shoulders dropped. That got her. She paused for a long while, thinking.

"You're right." She sighed. "It's important to keep your word." All of her energy seemed to be gone again. If my mom was a balloon, then I'd popped it. "If it's that important to you, we can go to the game."

"Dad said he's going. I could go with him," I suggested.

Mom bit her lip and looked down at her hands.

"Abuela and Grandad could take us!" Maribel said, placing a hand on Mom's arm.

"We'll all go," Mom said looking up. "Family night at the football game. Let's do it." She smiled at me, but it was the same fake smile she'd given me when I said I didn't want to watch the movie the day before. I'd hurt her again.

I'll make things better with Mom tomorrow. It's just until I put the medallion back, I said to myself. But even as I had the thought, I knew it was probably another lie.

Chapter 8

Friday Night Lights

Everyone in Castillo Bay was out at the homecoming game that night. The clear October sky had filled with fat navy clouds that looked like the stuffing in one of those Build-A-Bear machines, and the lights around the stadium flickered on early as the sky got dark. Fans in their red and black Castillo Bay Pirates shirts filtered in through the ticket gate carrying their blankets and folding stadium seats. All of their conversations seemed to be about whether or not the officials would call the game off on account of the storm.

"Nah, there's no way they'll call it. Not a homecoming game! Not without lightning within five miles. Even then, I bet it'd better strike twice—they'll pretend they didn't see it the first time." Grandad laughed.

I chuckled awkwardly, conscious all the time of the medallion I'd put around my neck before we left the house, tucked under my T-shirt and hoodie. My plan was to meet up with JC and Marcos, go slip it in the keeper's house mail slot, and be done with it. I looked past the field to the lighthouse tower in the distance. The beam from the beacon was dim, but the defiant lighthouse stood tall against the clouds that crowded in around it, sending the light out in circles anyway. It would take us a few minutes to get over there and a few minutes to get back, but we could make it.

A woman was announcing the homecoming court over the loudspeaker and girls in glittering gowns were parading out onto the field, escorted by their parents. With the wind whistling against the microphone, it was hard to understand anything the woman was saying. For a moment, something else took over the speakers. A man's cheesy charismatic radio voice softened by static fuzz. "*Ladies and gents, put your hands together for your Castillo Bay Pirates!*" the crackling voice said. Distant muted applause washed against my ears like waves on the shore as a complete team of boys in leather helmets and three-quarter-length breeches ran onto the field. Their jerseys looked like sweaters, tan with big red knit numbers.

"That's a cool thing they're doing. I've never seen that," I said to Mom, gesturing to the field. "Are those like old uniforms or something for homecoming?"

"What are we looking at?" Mom asked absently, looking out at the field and then back at me before being distracted by the woman next to her.

"Christina, you're here! That's so great. Good for you!" the woman said, tucking her hair behind an ear with a big red dangly number 34 earring before going on to chat about her son, who was on the team. Fan gear covered the woman from head to toe, ornamented with red and black sequins and tassels. "You'll be wearing one of these before we know it!" the woman said to Mom, pointing at the button on her shirt with a picture of her son in his uniform and winking at me.

Mom laughed politely and put her arm around me. "It was good to see you, Susan," she said. The woman gave an energetic wave and pushed through the crowd to find a seat.

"You can play football someday if you want to, Ian, but you don't have to. I'll be proud of you either way," Mom said quietly.

"You don't need a button?" I joked.

"Only if it would match my outfit." Mom tugged on her old red pirate sweatshirt that she always used to wear when we all went to games as a family. I noticed that she looked uncomfortable and out of place even though going to football games used to be one of her favorite things to do. Come to think of it, we hadn't been to a single football game ever since she and Dad split. When I saw Mom glance up at the clouds, I knew she was hoping lightning would strike so the game would be over before it started, and we could all go home. Suddenly, I wanted that for her too, but then I felt the weight of the medallion around my neck, and I said a silent prayer for the storm to hold off. Something told me the medallion was the reason for all of these strange things I'd been seeing. *I've got to get this thing back where it belongs.*

Back on the field, all the football players were gone except one who stood on the fifty yard line looking right at me. He opened his mouth to speak, but I couldn't hear what he was saying. I squinted my eyes, staring at him as he tried again. "Help me," he mouthed. My jaw dropped. I looked around to see if anyone else noticed, but everyone was just carrying on about their business as if everything was normal. "Help me," he mouthed again. I gripped the rusty metal railing along the front of the stands. *How? How can I help you?*

I blinked, and he was gone. In his place, a girl in a hot pink dress was touching the tiara on her head to great applause from the stands. The voice on the loudspeaker was a woman again. It was like the announcement about the football players never happened. The hair stood up on the back of my neck. These things I kept seeing were getting worse. It couldn't be an accident. The medallion burned hot against my chest. It was getting heavier by the second, pulling me down like an anchor. I couldn't wait to get rid of this thing.

Maribel ran over to one of the high school cheerleaders and exchanged a few dollars for a program, her red bow bobbing through the crowd back to us as we walked up the steps to find a seat in the stands. A couple of rough old guys in rubber waders and galoshes strolled slowly between us, and I almost shouted at Maribel to look where she was going as she headed right for them. But as I watched, her red bow filtered through them like a hand waving through smoke. I stopped in my tracks, gawking at them. So out of place. They turned their heads to stare at me as they kept creeping slowly forward and disappeared into the crowd.

"Don't stare at the cheerleaders," Maribel yelled louder than she needed to. She always had trouble regulating her voice level in a crowd.

"Shut up," I said, quickly looking back down. My ears burned as the cheerleaders giggled. Why did Maribel have to be so embarrassing?

"There's nothing wrong with finding the cheerleaders pretty, Ian." My *abuela* patted my leg as we sat down. "You're a handsome young man, and it's perfectly normal to notice girls more at this age."

I'm gonna throw up. I thought. *I'm actually going to vomit right here in front of everyone. The medallion will fall off my neck when I hurl, and everyone will know I'm a thief and a baby.*

"Can I go find my friends?"

"Well, it's pretty crowded." Mom fidgeted with the tattered hem of her sweatshirt.

"We said we'd meet by the concession stand," I told her. "Please, let me go."

Biting her lip, Mom glanced around again. "All right, but let's make a deal. Back here by fourth quarter, okay?"

I nodded as guilt seeped into my already nervous stomach.

"Let me get you some cash." She reached into her purse.

Maribel tugged at her sleeve. "Mom, can I go buy some snacks?"

She nodded and dug through her purse, handing me a ten and Mari a wadded-up five. "Make sure you watch the halftime show. I hear the drum line is excellent this year." Mom had been a band nerd in high school. Clarinet player. So she always went on about the marching band at halftime.

"Okay, thanks," I said hurriedly. "See you fourth quarter." I started down the steps, my hand on my chest to keep the medallion from swinging under my shirt, but Mom stopped me.

"Ian," she shouted. "Take your sister."

You've got to be kidding me.

"Yay!" Maribel hopped up and skipped down the steps to join me.

I opened my mouth to protest but stopped when I saw someone in a ball cap that looked like Dad sitting a few rows up and over. Laughing and drinking a beer. I did a double take. That couldn't be Dad. There was some blond lady in tiny cutoff shorts and cowboy boots wrapped around him whispering something in his ear. Her hair. Was that the hair I—

"Let's go!" Maribel pulled my arm down the stairs. A *tip-a-tip-a-tap* rang out on the metal stands as we hopped down.

Abuela groaned and held the program over her head.

"Oh, it's just a little rain," Grandad said. "Mark my words. Two lightning strikes in five miles or they won't call it."

****

"You brought your *sister*," Marcos whined.

"Calm down, she just wants some Frito pie," I said, stepping in line behind a bunch of high school kids.

"Hurry up," said JC. "My *tia* is only working the concession stand until halftime, and then she'll be looking for me."

I kicked at the dirt with my shoe, wet in spots where the rain had made marks before fading back into the clouds. "Well, you're the reason we're in this mess in the first place, so maybe you can both just chill." I was so mad that my voice cracked when I said it, and I was talking louder than I meant to. I glanced at the high school kids, hoping they didn't notice.

"What mess?" Maribel asked.

I turned around. "Nothing," I signed.

"What mess?" she persisted, signing back.

"I said nothing!" I signed.

"What do you need, honey?" JC's *tia* threw a towel over her shoulder as she spoke.

"Uh, one Frito pie and two Dr Peppers." I handed her my ten.

"Aren't you going to eat?" Maribel signed.

63

"Leave me alone. Take your dinner and go back to Mom," I signed.

"Here." JC's *tia* handed my change to me, acting annoyed that we were holding up the line.

"I want to stay with you!" Maribel shouted.

People were craning their necks to look at us.

I took Maribel by the arm and pulled her to the picnic tables. "You can't, okay? You keep yelling things and embarrassing me! Me and my friends have stuff we want to do. We don't need some little kid tagging along."

Maribel's big kitten eyes started to water.

"Frito pie!" someone shouted.

I let out a sigh and walked back up to the window to get Maribel's dinner and our drinks, but when I turned back around, she was gone.

"Maribel! Maribel?" I knew it was stupid to shout. She wouldn't be able to hear me in this crowd.

"Dude, just let her go. We've gotta get to the lighthouse," JC said under his breath.

I stood there holding the food and trying to pick out her red bow, but it was impossible in the sea of red and black. It was like the world's worst game of *Where's Waldo*. I set the Frito pie down on the picnic table and reached into my back pocket for my phone.

"I'll eat that," Marcos said, picking up the red and white paper basket and digging in to the meat and cheese covered chips.

I started to text my mom to tell her that Maribel was headed her way, but then I saw the sock hop couple again. They were sitting at the picnic tables. Drinking that same stupid milkshake. I shoved my phone back in my pocket and walked over to them.

"What are you doing here? Stop following me!" I

shouted. "Why are you wearing those clothes? They don't even sell milkshakes at the concession stand!"

The couple froze. Bewildered, they peered up at me, turned back and locked eyes with each other, and then looked back up at me again.

"Great catch by number 32. First down!"

The couple dissolved into thin air like mist in the wind with another wave of applause from the stands.

"Who asked about milkshakes?" A couple of high school girls scanned the snack area and started giggling. "Are you okay, kid?" one of them asked.

JC ran over and tugged me back by the arm. "Sorry, ladies, we just really wanna improve the menu around here. Really mad about the lack of options!"

I stared at the empty spot on the bench of the wooden picnic table where the couple had been. "You didn't see those people drinking a milkshake?" I asked JC.

"Dude, you're acting crazy." Marcos grabbed Maribel's Dr Pepper with his cheesy Frito pie fingers. "You gonna drink this?"

Behind us, the girls were still giggling and staring at me like I was some kind of freak.

"Let's go put this thing back where it belongs," I said to JC and Marcos. "I think it's making me crazy."

Chapter 9

Storm Clouds and Ghost Pirates

"Touchdown, Castillo Bay Pirates!" The announcer's voice rattled the chain-link fence as the three of us slipped out of the visitor gate and snuck past the visiting team's buses parked along the curb. Second quarter was just about to begin. The Castillo Bay Pirates were up 7-0. But I wasn't worried about the stadium lights behind me. I was looking ahead across the hazy navy sky to the lighthouse. We bolted across the dirt fields and city blocks toward the mystifying beacon that seemed to be pulling me toward it like a magnet.

"Does the light look different to you?" I asked JC as we ran.

"I don't know," he panted. JC had never been much of an athlete. "I guess it's more purple than usual?"

"Maybe it's because of the storm clouds," Marcos shouted.

BA-BA-BUM. As if on cue, thunder shook the sky, and the dark clouds grew in swirls above us.

"Hey, can we walk now? That Frito pie is gonna come right back up if we keep running."

Marcos stopped to hold on to his side. Big red circles had formed on his cheeks, and he was sweating like a pig.

JC stopped too and put his hands on his knees,

bending over to catch his breath. I wasn't tired, but the two of them looked like they were dying. Neither of them had played sports very much. It was part of why they didn't mind hanging out with me when I quit football and all my athletic friends turned their backs on me.

"We're almost there, guys. I can see the water."

The waves in the bay were growing taller as they rolled against the shore. We walked toward the lighthouse without speaking for a while, and my thoughts drifted back to the football players, the disappearing sailors, and the sock hop couple.

No one else saw them. I couldn't lie to myself anymore. *They were ghosts. I've been seeing ghosts.* I hadn't seen ghosts my whole life, and all of a sudden, they were everywhere. Ever since…I placed a hand absently on the bump where the medallion was. Somehow, I'd started seeing these ghosts when I'd gotten the medallion.

"Guys, I'm sorry I said you were stupid. I think you were right. I think…"

I looked up at the light from the beacon in the lighthouse and the rotating ray that it cast out across the ocean. Just below it, the porch light was on at the keeper's house. Not purple, but golden. Warm. Inviting. Just a few more steps, and I could slip the medallion in the mail slot. I'd get it off my neck and out of my life and everything would be okay.

"Why are we even running? The lighthouse isn't going anywhere. Just slow down." The red spots on Marcos's cheeks had spread to his whole face, and his black hair was matted around his head like a wet mop.

A whistle. *"Off sides. Five-yard penalty."* Snippets of the voice from the stadium in the distance pushed in with the wind at our backs. But just like before, something interrupted the announcer's voice. This time it sounded like a sea shanty. I stopped and looked around.

"Do you guys hear that?" I asked.

JC and Marcos stopped too, looking at each other like they thought I was crazy. But then Marcos grabbed my arm. "Dude, look out there!" He pointed to the ocean.

Far out into the bay, illuminated every ten seconds or so by a beam of passing purple light from the lighthouse, was a crew of sailors hovering just above the water. They were trudging toward the lighthouse like men against the wind, some holding onto their hats, some waving pistols or swords in the air, and some dragging what looked like chains or seaweed. They moved in slow motion like every step was a chore. And carrying over the wind and waves, they were singing:

Golden, stolen, dripping with blood
Bones and truth buried deep in the mud
Golden, stolen, heavy with strife
Lies that claim each sailor's life
Golden, stolen, dripping with blood
Bones and truth buried deep in the mud
For ears that hear, the finder's fee
Is a sailor's life for the truth set free

The man leading the slow march toward the lighthouse began to materialize through the mist, starting with his white captain's hat.

"Guys, I know who that is," I said. "I saw a picture of him in the research Mrs. Rodriguez gave us! It's Captain Ellis Larsen." It was the man from the article online who'd been leaning on the hull of the ship that crashed in 1922.

"Who?" JC panted.

"He was the captain of that ship that went on an expedition to Colombia to find the medallion, and then died and was lost at sea." The next clap of thunder shook my spine. These sailors and that captain were the ghosts from the sunken ship *Olivia*.

"Those are freakin' pirate ghosts, man!" Marcos shouted.

"Just like my *tia* said!" JC's voice was quivering. "We've gotta get outta here!"

I staggered backward. Fear clutched my chest like I'd felt last year when we went to an amusement park on our school field trip and my friends talked me into riding the tallest roller coaster even though I hate heights. That feeling after the car had clicked up and clicked up and was tilting slowly over the top loop, about to send us plunging downward, and there was nothing I could do to stop it. The same feeling I'd had when Mom and Dad sat me and Maribel down at the kitchen table to tell us they'd be getting a divorce. Even though I knew it was coming, something about the way the car was about to rush forward, the way I didn't know where it would go or if I'd survive, made me want to cry and squeeze my eyes shut and throw up at the same time.

"No!" I shouted above the howl of the wind and the chant of the sailors. "We've got to return the medallion. I know it sounds crazy, but I think…I think it's the reason for the ghosts. I think there's some sort of curse, and it won't be fixed until we put the medallion back where it belongs."

Marcos and JC plodded beside me to the keeper's house, if not a little behind me. We got to the pathway leading to the porch, and I laughed at this sticker in the dirt that said, "Vote for Mayor Juarez." Just a few days ago, this had been a fun little field trip. Now it was a house for ghost pirates.

JC's shaking hand grabbed my shoulder. "I-I-Ian, look up at the lighthouse window."

I followed his gaze to the top of the lighthouse as swirling booms from the sky echoed out over the shore in a series of whooshes. Someone was standing in the window near the top of the tower. Someone who was glaring at us with eyes that almost glowed in the darkness. A flash of lightning lit up the sky, as well as the face that belonged to the eyes. It was the man from the shadows.

I stood for a moment, as still as the lighthouse in the storm. If he was the one who started this curse, well, he could have it. I broke away from his gaze and looked back at the keeper's house.

"Come on, guys," I said. "We're almost there."

But there was no answer.

I turned around to look for my friends, and in another sweep of light from the lighthouse, I could see them running sloppily back toward the stadium. Away from the lighthouse. Away from me.

As I watched after them, I knew I could catch up. I could start running now and pass them. It wasn't the direction I wanted to go, but at least I wouldn't be alone.

"Cowards!" I shouted after them, my voice lost in the wind. *No*, I thought. *I'm here, and I'm going to do this*. I could hear the ghost sailors chanting behind me. I could feel the watchful eyes from the lighthouse tower boring into me. I reached under my shirt, clutched the medallion, and stomped up the path to the keeper's house porch, glaring defiantly at the eyes in the tower.

Just a few more steps and I could be done with all of

this. Get back to the game. Back to normal.

"Well, hello there, young man," a friendly voice said.

I jumped and took a step back. I'd been so fixated on the man in the lighthouse window that I hadn't been looking in front of me where a thin man wearing suspenders and a bow tie was smiling at me and leaning on a rake.

"I-I...hello," I stammered, looking around and then back toward the stadium. I could just make out the distant voice of the announcer and the cheering of the crowd.

"That's halftime, folks!"

"Stanley," he answered, holding out his hand. "Stanley Jones."

"Ian," I said, shaking his hand. It was icy cold.

"Why aren't you at the game with your friends, Ian?" Stanley asked. His warm smile spread slowly with a kind of patience that reminded me of a grandfather, but he looked like he couldn't be older than my dad.

"Those aren't my friends." I glanced back and tried to make out the figures of JC and Marcos running off toward the safety of the stadium.

"Well, you're probably right about that." Stanley stood up from his rake to resume pulling leaves across the lawn. "That isn't always an easy lesson to learn, though, is it?" He looked meaningfully up at the lighthouse for a moment and then back at me.

"There's someone up there, isn't there? In the lighthouse? I thought it was closed to tours, and I..." I fumbled with the medallion beneath my sweatshirt.

"Well, son, you're right about that, too. The lighthouse *is* closed to tours. All these storms. All this time. She's wearing down on the inside even if she looks all right from the outside. Just isn't safe for outsiders." The man finished raking one pile and moved across the yard to start on another. It seemed strange that he was raking leaves in the face of a windy thunderstorm. Strange that he moved so calmly and deliberately in the midst of the chaos that surrounded us.

"But there *is* someone up there. That'd be ol' Malachi. He hangs around here from time to time. Likes to look out over the ocean. Likes to watch the…well, the sailors."

"Ghost sailors," I said, sounding more confident than I felt.

Stanley looked up at me with a twinkle in his eye. "Right again, Ian. Those sailors coming toward us are ghosts. Don't you worry about those cranky ghost sailors, though. They can't come ashore as long as that beacon is burning. That reliable ol' girl has kept her light shining for a hundred years, and protects us all when she does."

Towering above us, the lighthouse stood strong against the darkness. Light ran in measured beams across the shore.

" 'Course, there's a change in the air. Something is different this time."

"Different?"

"Mhmm. Something is missing. Don't you worry, though. We'll set it right."

"How do we do that?" I asked in a panic.

"You don't have to do anything. That's my responsibility. You know, you remind me a little bit of my son, Thomas. Smart. Good kid." Stanley finished his pile, propped the rake on the wall, and dusted his hands on his trousers.

Before I could ask Stanley any more questions, my phone buzzed in my pocket. When I took it out, I had five missed calls from my mom and a series of text messages that started with "Where are you," had something about Maribel crying in the middle, and ended with "GET BACK UP HERE NOW!" That text message scared me more than the ghost pirates. Or ghost sailors. Or…

"I-I'm sorry, sir. I have to…" But when I looked up, Stanley was gone.

CRACK. Another flash of lightning illuminated the sky, and thunder boomed. With the lightning, the porch lights flickered off, and I was left in complete darkness.

I remembered what Grandad said, that if lightning struck twice in five miles, the game would be over. Everyone would be looking for me. *I'm going to be in so much trouble.* I staggered backward and turned to run toward the stadium, phone buzzing in my hand again as I ran.

Brassy blends of trumpet horns and the rolling *pit-a-pat* of the drums drifted through the air toward me from the stadium, slowly becoming louder than the distant echo of the sailors chanting, *Golden, stolen, dripping with blood. Treasure and truth buried deep in the mud. Till then the sea will hide our bones. Dark in the depths of the Davy Jones.*

Chapter 10

Blueberry Muffins

Never in my life had I seen my mom so mad. After I'd found Mom, Maribel, and my grandparents in the huge mass of people spilling out to their cars, it had been one long lecture from my mother that didn't end until my head finally hit the pillow.

"Someday you'll wake up, Ian! You'll realize that *friends* like JC and Marcos are not good for you. They're about as loyal as a seagull on the shore. They'll leave your handful of bread for a bigger handful, and whenever you run out, you'll never see them again. Your family is forever. Your *sister*, your sister is your friend for life, son. You have her, and she's supposed to trust that she can count on you. You can't just run off and leave her because you feel like it!" She went on and on, more things like how I'd let her down. It didn't seem to matter how many times I said, "Yes, ma'am" or "I'm sorry."

"You didn't even watch the marching band! You know I wanted to talk to you about that! *Where were you?*"

It made it even worse that I hadn't answered my phone, and that I couldn't tell her where I had been. But worst of all was the fact that, after all that, all the trouble I was in, I still hadn't returned the stupid medallion. I turned it over in my hands, running my thumb along the bumps on the outside. The front looked like the smooth face of a sun. I flipped it over to the back, which was full of shapes and symbols I didn't recognize. It was almost hypnotizing. Drawing me in…

"Ian." Maribel poked her head into the room.

I shoved the medallion under my mattress. "What?" I snapped. "Can't you knock?"

"Sorry, I…I just wanted to say that I'm sorry that you got in trouble."

"That *you got me* in trouble, you mean? Get out of my room, Maribel!"

Maribel skulked out and gently closed the door. I waited for the door to click shut and flopped onto my bed, exhausted, but completely aware that I wouldn't be getting any sleep.

I had another sleepless night ahead of me, full of worries, ghosts, and curses.

Every time I closed my eyes, visions of the night's events took over. The marching crew of ghost sailors, or nice old Mr. Jones leaning on his rake, completely unafraid of the storm or the ghosts, or any of the trouble around us. I decided he was my solution. He would understand. During the night, I made a plan. I'd go find Stanley at the keeper's house during the festival and give the medallion to him. He would help me. The whole festival would take place right there between the keeper's house and the football field, so I could slip away and back in a matter of minutes.

It wouldn't be fun to admit to Stanley that I'd had the medallion the whole time we were talking last night, but it would be a relief to get it off my chest. Literally.

If I'm even allowed to go to the festival, I thought, remembering something in the middle of Mom's rant about being grounded for life.

When I sat at the breakfast table with Mom and Maribel the next morning, it was clear that Mom hadn't slept much either. She set out a box of Ghost Berries cereal along with a jug of milk and plopped into her seat at the table with nothing but a cup of hot coffee and a frown.

"You know that I have to work the bakery booth at the festival again this year." Mom held her coffee mug with both hands and took a long drink. "Abuela and Grandad have some things to do this morning but they're free in the afternoon. I think the Lighthouse Preservation Society is having a silent auction or…" Mom got up to pour herself another cup of coffee. "Today I'd like you both to come with me to the festival. You can hang out in the bakery booth until Abuela and Grandad can stop by at lunch."

"Yay, I love the festival. Thanks, Mom," Maribel said, a little less enthusiastic than usual but still annoying for eight in the morning. Her eyes were puffy. She smiled at me weakly and dug into her cereal.

"Ian, we will need to continue our conversation from last night later, but I will say I am sorry I got so upset with you."

I put my spoon down. "Mom, I'm sorry too. I—"

Mom reached out and put her hand on mine. "Let's just set it aside and enjoy the festival today, okay?"

I nodded, picked up my spoon, and finished my cereal, looking at the cartoon ghosts on the box a little differently than I ever had before.

The morning air at the festival grounds was my favorite kind of cold, the kind that carried the ocean air and settled it in drops on my jacket but didn't freeze my fingers or burn my eardrums. The storm from the night before had left puddles in the hollows of the ground and settled the sky in a kind of pale blue-gray that sat somewhere between morning mist and fog. Dewy grass and wet dirt burrowed in sandy canyons under my lawn chair as I pushed it to the back of the pop-up tent next to boxes of baked goods in cellophane bags. Maribel sat in her own chair, snuggled up in a fuzzy blanket with a book about pirates.

Hammers on nails rang out across the crisp air, punctuating laughter and morning greetings as volunteer groups assembled a stage for the pageants and contests. Across the field, I could see my grandparents arranging baskets on long wooden picnic tables for the Lighthouse Preservation Society silent auction. People were starting to mill around leisurely, stopping here and there to peruse the booths that were already set up. Looking around, I couldn't tell which festival visitors were real live people, and which ones were ghosts. Even though the festivities hadn't officially started yet, Mom had already sold enough muffins to dig into the box beside me for more to replace them on the display table.

"I can help, Mom." I grabbed a few wrapped bread slices and set them out on the table, too.

Mom considered me for a moment and handed me a cloth apron with three pockets.

"Why don't you grab a few ones for change from the cash box? You can help me with the customers."

"Okay." I bent my head down to get the money.

"What's this?" she said, tugging at the chain on my neck.

"Nothing," I said, straightening up quickly and pulling the collar of my jacket up over the chain.

"Something Dad gave me on Thursday," I lied.

Mom's eyebrows furrowed in confusion, and her eyes lingered on my neck.

"So, how much is everything?" I asked quickly, tying the little apron around my waist.

Mom picked up a price sheet from one of the boxes. "Everything on the front table is two dollars. I posted the price sheet for boxes of cookies and pies out front. Let's put another one here." She propped the sign on the table surrounded by cakes and pies in brown boxes sealed with Castillo Bay Cookie Palace stickers.

"Seems easy enough," I said. "Did you make all this, Mom?"

She straightened a stack of pies. "Most of it."

"That's a lot," I said, looking around at the full booth. *No wonder she's so tired all the time.*

Mom grinned and placed her hands on her hips. "Let's hope it all sells."

Working with my mom kept me so busy that I forgot about the ghosts. She seemed thrilled that everything was selling so well, and for the moment, our argument was a distant memory. I decided that as long as somebody had money to pay for their baked goods, I didn't care if they were ghosts or not. I even forgot about the medallion under my T-shirt for a while until Miss Jones approached with another lady wearing a business suit. At the sight of her, I knocked over the price sign and a whole pile of muffins.

Is that other lady some kind of lawyer or detective? I kept Miss Jones in sight as I tried to reorganize the mess I'd made of the table. *Did she see the video footage from our field trip? Is she coming to tell my mom?*

"Ian, isn't it?" Miss Jones said pleasantly.

I searched her face for a hint of anger or judgment. *Does she know I have the medallion?*

"Yes, ma'am," I said. "Thank you again for the coin. I really enjoyed the tour of the keeper's house."

"I'm so glad you did! This is my friend, Miss Ortiz. She's from Bogotá, Colombia, where much of the treasure you saw on Wednesday came from."

"*Hola,* Ian." Miss Ortiz shook my hand.

"*Bienvenidos a* Castillo Bay," I answered, hoping that Miss Ortiz didn't notice my palms were sweaty.

"*Gracias!*" Miss Ortiz said enthusiastically. "Clever boy!"

I blushed. "My *abuela* taught me Spanish."

My mom joined us and exchanged a poppyseed muffin for a few dollars with Miss Jones.

"What brings you here from Bogotá, Miss Ortiz?" my mom asked after introducing herself.

"Call me Camila, please," she said, smiling. "Desiree has invited me to look at the artifacts on display at the keeper's house. Much of Colombia's heritage and many artifacts were taken by people who plundered our graves and sites in the name of 'exploration' long ago or with archaeology as a hobby. There is an initiative to return those artifacts to Colombia where they rightfully belong, or in some cases, leave them in the current museum and update the tags that identify them. Desiree and I will be going through the artifacts over the next few weeks to determine the right way to deal with the items that have been salvaged from the ship *Olivia,* which was full of stolen Muisca artifacts."

My mom commented, "Oh, that must be complicated!"

"It can be," Miss Jones answered, studying me as

she spoke. "But it's the right thing to do. We should return the stolen treasure to Colombia if the people there want it back."

I felt like she could see right through my shirt to the medallion beneath it.

"But we didn't steal it," I protested.

"No, we didn't," Miss Jones said gently. "But if we keep it when we know it was taken unfairly, isn't that the same as stealing? That's why I reached out to Miss Ortiz. It's *her* decision what we do with the treasure."

"I guess that makes sense."

Miss Ortiz bought a slice of chocolate banana bread from my mom and broke off a bite. "This is delicious!" she said before turning back to me. "Don't worry, young man. We try to be fair and considerate. If our museum has plenty of similar artifacts to the ones you have at the keeper's house, we will allow it to remain with a tag identifying that it is on loan from the people of Colombia."

"Oh, that is nice!" my mom said.

"I am disappointed, though, to hear that the Moon Goddess medallion is missing. That artifact is definitely worth examining." Miss Ortiz took another bite of the chocolate bread.

I shifted uncomfortably from one foot to the other. *Give it to them. Give it to them right now. Tell them you didn't steal it, but you found it.*

"Hello, Desiree. Christina." Mayor Juarez approached the booth. "It's a fine day for a festival!"

Miss Jones and Mom exchanged a subtle eye roll.

"Good morning, Mayor. Would you like some breakfast? We've got muffins, bread, danishes, and—"

"Oh no, no. I could never. Counting my carbs, you

know!" He placed a flat hand on his stomach and flashed a smile at Miss Ortiz. "Julian Juarez," he said, holding out his hand to shake hers. "I'm the mayor of Castillo Bay."

"Nice to meet you, Mayor Juarez. Camila Ortiz." She shook his hand with a polite but tight-lipped smile.

"Well, we'd better get going. I'd like Camila to see all that the festival has to offer," Miss Jones said quickly. "Lots to explore!"

"Thank you for the delicious bread, Christina," Miss Ortiz said to my mom. "I'll have to visit your bakery again before I go."

"I hope you do!" my mom said.

The women left the booth and headed toward the rest of the festival, but Miss Jones turned around before they were out of sight. "I hope to see you back at the lighthouse soon, Ian. You're welcome there any time."

She waded out into the crowd with Miss Ortiz and washed away before she could hear me say "Thank you."

Mayor Juarez looked after the women for a moment before turning back to my mom.

"Who was that woman with Desiree? She's not a Castillo Bay citizen."

"I'm not sure," Mom said as she wiped down the table between them. "A friend from out of town, I guess."

He squinted his eyes, studying my mother for a moment, and then cast a glance back after the women again. "I hope it isn't another buyer for the lighthouse. The city council and the society are finally ready to accept my proposal, and I don't need out-of-town competition complicating things."

"I'm sure your proposal will be accepted...if it's

really the best thing for Castillo Bay and the lighthouse," my mom answered.

"If?" Mayor Juarez squared up his shoulders and straightened his jacket. "Of course, my proposal is the best thing for the town."

Mom kept wiping at the table without looking up.

"Well. I have things to see to. Give my regards to Blake and Ashlee," he snapped as he turned to walk away.

My mother's arm tensed, and she squeezed the rag before dropping it back into the box below the table. She opened her mouth as if to speak, but closed it again.

"Why didn't you tell him who the lady was?" I asked my mom once the mayor was out of sight.

Maribel looked up from her book as if she wanted to hear the answer too.

"It wasn't for me to tell. Miss Jones could have shared that information with him if she felt he needed to know, and clearly, she didn't. Mayor Juarez is so concerned with his bid to buy the lighthouse and turn it into a big tourist attraction, and the treasure definitely brings tourists. He probably wouldn't want us to give back the medallion or any of the treasure, even if we *had* obtained it unethically."

"Unethically?" I asked.

"It means if we got it in a way that wasn't morally right. Like by stealing and lying."

My cheeks and ears grew hot. "But didn't you just lie to Mayor Juarez?" I asked. "What's the difference?"

Mom's jaw tensed again. She picked up her phone to look at the time. Behind her, Maribel shuffled in her seat and pretended to be interested in her book.

"I'd like to buy a muffin," said the deepest, gruffest

voice I'd ever heard.

When I turned around, I was face-to-big-ruddy-face with the man from the shadows.

"I'm s-sorry, sir?" My voice wavered. I might as well have been two inches tall beneath the hovering figure of the giant man. Two of me could fit in one leg of his rubber yellow overalls. Scraggly, straw-yellow hairs squiggled out around his square jaw and patchy red face. His beady, bloodshot eyes had dark circles under them that made it look like he'd never slept. Like he'd been restlessly staring at people from the shadows for years. I remembered the way Stanley had shrugged his shoulders beneath the watchful glare of the man. *Malachi*, I told myself. *Stanley called him Malachi.*

"I'd like a blueberry muffin," Malachi said, his voice somewhere between a growl and a rumble.

I shuddered and took a step back. "We're all out of blueberry. Sorry."

Malachi's eyes narrowed.

"Well...bye!" I smiled quickly.

"Ian!" My mom stepped in. "Of course we have blueberry muffins. So sorry, sir. Here you are. Baked them myself." Mom placed a cellophane bag with a muffin in Malachi's massive hand. "Two dollars please."

Malachi grunted and glared as he dug in his pocket for cash and set it on the table. A dollar and four quarters. Tongue trapped in my throat, I watched as the last quarter spun in a slow circle before dropping flat on the table.

"Thanks! Enjoy the festival!" my mom said cheerfully.

"And you do the same," he said, his scary eyes still boring into me.

He picked up his muffin and started to whistle. My ears pricked up at the tune. It was the sea shanty the pirate ghosts sang in the storm the night before. Malachi turned around slowly and walked away, whistling all the while. He unwrapped the muffin as he worked through the bustling crowd, peering back and forth at the booths that were busily interacting with festivalgoers. He paused to gnaw on the muffin and watch a bunch of kids take turns playing whack-a-mole.

"That was so weird," I muttered, finally remembering to exhale.

"I know, right?" Mom agreed, placing her hands on her hips. "I would have pegged him as more of a 'steak and eggs for breakfast' kinda guy."

Chapter 11

The Tower

I was pretty shaken up for the rest of the morning after seeing Malachi again and speaking with him for the first time.

"Are you okay, Ian?" my mom asked me.

"Yes. Yeah, absolutely," I lied. "I'm just excited to look around." I was more ready than ever to go put the medallion back where it belonged.

Mom considered me for a moment. "You know what? You've been super helpful today. And very responsible. I think I can trust you to walk around the festival without an adult."

"What? Really!" Excitement and relief washed over me. *This is perfect! I can go put the medallion back without having to explain to anyone what I'm doing.*

"Yes. Let's set some ground rules," Mom said.

"Anything!"

"Turn your phone on loud. And answer on the first ring if I call. Return every text I send you."

I took my phone out of my pocket and switched it to loud. "No problem."

"Be back here by nine so you can help me pack up, and then we'll all watch the fireworks together."

"Deal," I said, trying not to bob up and down. I was so ready to sail off toward the lighthouse.

"And take your sister with you."

And just like a ship dropping its anchor, my heart sank. At the back of the tent, Maribel was still absorbed in her book.

"But Mom!"

"Take Maribel with you." Mom's tone told me the discussion was over. "And don't ditch her this time."

My heart landed somewhere in the bottom of my stomach. "Okay," I finally gave in.

I went over to Maribel and bumped her shoulder. She looked up at me hesitantly.

"Wanna go walk around with me?" I signed.

A big, wide-eyed smile spread across her face. "Yes!" she said, closing her book and hopping up. "Can we play carnival games?" she signed.

I nodded. "First, I'd like to go to the keeper's house, though," I signed.

Maribel made a face at me that I didn't understand, and then she nodded and reached for her jacket.

"Okay, Mom, we're going to go exploring," I said. "Don't worry, my phone is on loud. I promise I'll answer your texts."

"Ian, wait," Mom said, fishing in her back pocket. "Here's some cash. Thank you for your help this morning. You earned it."

Mom didn't know I'd only helped her to distract me from seeing all the ghosts. To distract me from worrying about the medallion. I felt a little guilty as I accepted the praise and the money from her hand. "Thanks, Mom."

"You're welcome, son," she said, going back to restocking the cookie table.

Maribel and I started out of the tent toward the keeper's house. "Ian," Mom shouted after me, "I love you! Be nice to your sister!"

Everyone around us turned to see who she was talking to. I couldn't get out of there fast enough.

"Come on, Maribel," I said, tugging on her elbow and ducking down through the crowd.

I kept an eye out for Malachi as we meandered through the booths and games toward the keeper's house, but he was nowhere in sight. Other than asking for cotton candy on the way, Maribel wasn't talking very much. *It's probably pretty tough to hear anything with all the background noise*, I decided.

When we got to the keeper's house, a girl was locking the front door and putting up a sign.

"Excuse me," I asked the girl. "Could we go in?"

"Sorry, kid. We're all going to help with the silent auction and benefit lunch at the festival," the girl said. "Don't worry, we'll be back to resume tours at two p.m." She tapped the sign. *Closed*, it said. *Come back at two*.

"Okay, thanks," I said, feeling defeated.

The girl gave an impatient wave of her hand as she hustled off down the pathway toward the festival, carrying a bunch of bags bursting with rolls of paper, posters, and awkward wooden frames.

I let out a frustrated sigh. *One minute too late.*

"Why do you want to go in there so bad?" Maribel signed.

I hesitated. "I liked the tour the other day. There was some stuff I didn't get to see. I thought you'd like it too."

Maribel pursed her lips, studying me skeptically before finally signing back. "This doesn't have anything to do with the medallion, does it?"

"What?" I took a step back. Maribel stood blinking, waiting for my answer. I didn't know what to say.

87

"My friend Kenzie has a sister in your grade," Maribel said. "She told us someone stole a bunch of treasure and the whole class got in trouble."

"Maribel, I—"

"I saw you hiding something gold under your bed."

There was no point in keeping it from her now. I motioned for her to join me under a tree in the keeper's house yard near the tree where I'd met Stanley, and I told her the whole story. As I got to the end, I looked around us to make sure no one was nearby, and I slipped the medallion from beneath my T-shirt to show it to Maribel.

She gasped and looked up at me, reaching out to touch the medallion. I felt so relieved to finally tell someone, I thought I was going to cry.

"What are we going to do?" Maribel signed.

I tucked the medallion back under my shirt, already feeling like it wasn't quite as heavy as before.

"We?" I said. "You didn't do anything wrong. You don't have to be a part of this. It's my responsibility to make it right."

Maribel didn't hesitate. "I'm your sister. I want to help."

Maybe having Mari tag along isn't so bad after all, I thought.

I smiled at my sister and was about to thank her and come up with a plan when I saw a figure moving toward the lighthouse.

"Maribel, look," I signed, pointing to the tower. "That's Mr. Stanley! He's so nice. He can help us. You're going to love him."

Mr. Stanley had an armful of red roses, and he adjusted his bowtie as he paced toward the tower. He pulled open the door of the lighthouse tower and ducked inside.

Maribel and I ran the short distance from the front of the keeper's house to the lighthouse tower at the back, where the outside door to enter the tower was propped open with a rock. I looked back at my sister. "You're already doing better than JC and Marcos. They couldn't run more than ten steps without panting and whining. I bet you really are the best soccer player in your grade."

Maribel laughed, her eyes twinkling. "I won't turn and run off on you either."

I gently pushed the door open and stepped inside. Immediately, my nostrils were hit with the kind of smell you could only find in an old lighthouse. The air was thick with moisture and the cold salty smell of moldy concrete.

"Maybe Dad is right," Maribel said, looking around the circular ground floor room with a scrunched nose. "Maybe the Preservation Society should let his boss fix it up."

My sneakers squeaked against the cold concrete as I moved tentatively forward toward the metal steps around the outside of the circular room. Muffled footsteps moved quickly above us.

"Mr. Stanley?" I shouted. Maribel and I exchanged glances as we waited for a reply.

"Stanley?"

The concrete walls reverberated with the echo of my voice, "Stanley-anley-lee-lee," and a brick fell from the inside wall and shattered on the concrete beside Maribel's pink shoe. She jumped back and looked up at me.

"This isn't safe," I said. "We should get you out of here."

But as we made for the door, it slammed shut with a steely bang that echoed throughout the tunnel and sent another brick tumbling down from the walls beside us.

I pulled at the door and turned to Maribel. "It's locked."

Her eyes grew wide with fear. I looked around, trying to come up with a solution. I spotted the other door that led to the keeper's house, but when I pulled on that door, it was locked, too. I glanced upward again toward the echo of Stanley's footsteps.

"We've gotta talk to Stanley. He'll be able to let us out," I said.

Maribel looked fearfully up to the winding staircase.

"I'm sorry, Maribel," I said. "But the only way out is up. We can do it."

I took her hand, and we walked to the rusty railing together. I placed my other hand on the cold peeling metal and tested out the first step.

I turned back to my sister. "It's safe. It just looks a little sketchy."

"I trust you," she said, taking a step to follow me. Something about the way she said she trusted me, the way she was willing to follow me even though I'd been kind of a jerk to her lately, made me feel guilty. It made me feel sorry that I'd gotten so frustrated with her. It seemed like she was on my side, no matter what.

We continued taking careful steps up the cold metal stairs, the rusty mesh that covered the stairs creaking beneath our tennis shoes from time to time. A full walk around the inside perimeter of the lighthouse led us to the second floor. Small windows on either side looked out toward either the sea or back toward Castillo Bay. Maribel and I stopped to look out of both. I could see the festival from my window, and I wondered if this was the window where Malachi had been watching me from the night before. I placed my hand on the windowsill and found another wobbly brick. At first, I shoved it back, but then I changed my mind. I pulled on the brick. *CLINK.* A key had fallen by my shoe. I knelt down to pick it up and noticed that the key disturbed the dust that looked like it had been there for a really long time. There was no way Malachi could have been standing at this window. There would be big bootprints or something. All I could see was the scraped spot from the key and the imprint of my size seven sneakers.

"Look," I said to Maribel, holding up the key. "I think I found our way out."

Maribel looked at me with surprise.

"It just fell out of this hollowed-out brick," I said, looking under the brick before putting it back.

Maribel stared at the key for a moment, out of her window at the water for another moment, and then back at me. "I still think we should go to the top first. We're already here."

I shrugged my shoulders and tucked the key into my jeans pocket. It clinked against the commemorative coin Miss Jones had given me a few days ago that I had started carrying with me. Not all the kids had earned one of those. I guess it made me feel special. It was kind of like a good luck charm now. We kept climbing. On the third floor, there was another set of windows, and the tower grew more narrow, closing in on us. These bricks looked ready to crumble too, and I finally understood why they decided not to give tours in here. This thing looked fine from the outside, but on the inside, it was falling apart.

Finally, I stepped up the last set of metal mesh steps

to the very top of the lighthouse. The room was small, surrounded by windows with a large glass light about half my height in the middle. It was a special kind of light, called a Fresnel lens. We had learned about it in school. A guy named Augustin-Jean Fresnel had designed the glass to be cut a certain way so it wouldn't be so heavy and the light could shine farther out. Most lighthouses use LED lights like Mayor Juarez had suggested the lighthouse needed to get, but the glass was beautiful. Probably a hundred years old.

I could understand why they didn't want to replace it. Why they didn't want things to change.

Maribel stepped in after me, peering nervously out the window and stepping back to the center of the room. "Where is Stanley?"

"I don't know," I said. "I swear I saw him come in here." There was no exit in the top part of the tower. I looked around at the windows. We were pretty high up there, and when I looked in the direction of the festival, the people looked small enough to pick up between your fingers like little toy soldiers. I looked for a second exit or another stairwell, but there was only one way in or out. *If Stanley didn't come up here, where did he go?*

A child's laughter reverberated off the windowpanes like raindrops. I turned, thinking Mari must have found something funny, but she stood stone faced, gaping at the room. It didn't seem like she'd heard anything, and she sure wasn't laughing.

What's going on? Is it another ghost?

Attempting to appear unafraid, I pulled a chair from the wall for Maribel. "Here you go."

"Are we staying up here long?" She sat down slowly.

"No, but I'd like to look around for a minute. Figure some things out." I found an old brown leather journal lying on the floor. I picked it up and began to thumb through it.

"What's that?" she asked.

I handed the journal to Maribel and kept inspecting the room to see if there was anything else worth taking a look at. My eyes were drawn to the green wooden trim that ran all the way around the top of the lighthouse. It had the initials JSJ carved into the wood followed by tic marks in a long line across the green trim that circled around the top and almost met up with the beginning again.

"JSJ," I said, pointing to the letters and running my fingers across the surface of the wood where they'd been carved.

"Julian something Juarez?" Maribel suggested.

"Maybe. But why would he be up here?"

"First Mate Javenson," she said.

"Those letters aren't the same, Maribel," I said, looking back at the letters beneath my fingers.

"No, silly. This journal. It belonged to First Mate Javenson." Maribel held the journal up.

Scrawled across the front page was the name along with a series of dates and numbers. "The *Olivia*, 1922."

"The *Olivia* is that ship that went down in the big hurricane. It's the one they got all the treasure from. But why would the first mate's journal be up here?"

"I wonder if someone was using it to look at the stars or something. There are lots of sketches of the moon and stars and stuff." She handed me the journal with trembling fingers.

"I guess someone could have found it in the

wreckage. Or maybe it washed up on shore somehow." I flipped through the journal, looking at a handful of pages dedicated to documenting the moon cycle with some symbols I'd never seen before scrawled all over the page. "Hey, wait a second," I said, remembering the framed pages from the tour. "I've seen something like this before! Let's go back into the keeper's house."

Maribel shot up from the chair fast as lightning. I guess I hadn't noticed how scared she was. Maybe she was trying just as hard as I was to seem brave.

BOOM. As we made our way down the winding metal ladder, thunder shook the room around us, dropping a few more bricks from the walls. Maribel jumped down the steps more quickly to avoid the bricks and slipped, letting out a piercing scream.

I seized Maribel by the arm and pulled her back as crumbles of mortar sprinkled in front of her face. We were both chilled by the echo of bricks hitting the ground. I moved in front of my sister to protect her.

"Follow me. I'll keep you safe." I said it confidently, but I didn't know for sure that it was true. As we hurried down the rusty steps towards the doors at the bottom, I hoped the promise of our safety wasn't another lie.

Chapter 12

Symbols and Keys

The rain pattering against the outside of the tower echoed along with our footsteps creeping down the winding stairs. A ding came from my pocket and ricocheted against the bricks somewhere around the second level.

I took out my phone and clicked on the unread message from my mom.

—*Just checking in. The storm is getting pretty bad. You kiddos okay? Where are you?*—

—*We are at the keeper's house.*— I responded.

—*Why don't you stay in there until the rain passes?*— Mom texted back.

I gave her text a thumbs-up.

—*I love you. Be nice to your sister.*—

I started to text "I love you" back to her but deleted it. Then "I'm sorry that…" but I deleted that too. Instead, I just typed "*K*" and sent her a GIF of a pirate eating tacos.

"Mom's good for a while," I said, tucking my phone into my back pocket.

"Where are we going?" Maribel asked.

"I saw pages like the ones from the journal in picture frames above a desk in the keeper's house. They had English words next to the symbols that look like the ones in this journal."

We got to the bottom floor and tried the doors again. Still locked. I fumbled in my pocket for the key that I'd found and tried it in the door that led to the keeper's house hallway.

"Do you think the door closed from the wind?" Maribel asked, shrinking into the center of the room.

"Probably," I lied. I'd been asking myself the same question, but there was no way the wind moved the big rock that held that big steel door open.

Maribel looked unsatisfied with my answer but nodded and stepped in closer to me as I jiggled the key in the handle.

Maribel watched me take the key out and blow the dust off before trying again. "I get why someone would want to lock the tower to keep people from getting in, but why would they lock it so they couldn't get out?" She asked.

I slid the key back in and tried the doorknob again, this time able to turn it. The steely screech of the tumblers rotating reverberated in the empty concrete room, rain still thumping the outside walls. I pulled the door toward us and peered down the short hallway to another door. The white wood walls and small square windows on each side of the hallway echoed the white bricks and windows in the lighthouse. There was a long, thin, red and navy rug that ran the length of the hallway. I held the door for my sister and let her walk through first, but she looked back at me with those timid kitten eyes of hers. I took her hand, and we walked together to the next door. I heard something on the other side of the door click when we were inches away.

My cold, sweaty hand went to turn the handle. It was

stuck too.

"Another locked door!" Maribel moaned. "It seems like someone is trying really hard to keep us out of here."

I tried the key I'd used on the last door, but it wouldn't work. I used the hem of my shirt to rub off some of the rust, and I tried it again. The doorknob didn't budge. I tucked the key back into my pocket and looked around. "If there was a key hidden in the lighthouse, maybe there's a key hidden in the hallway."

Maribel raised an eyebrow but joined me in looking for a key anyway. I stood on tiptoes, trying to reach the top of the door frame, but I was too short. Mirabel looked under the rug.

Nothing.

"I don't think they hid a key," Maribel said, standing back and putting her hands in her pockets. "We should call Mom. She can have someone let us out."

"No. We can get out on our own." I knelt down to pull at the wooden planks with my fingers. I couldn't find a loose board on the floor or a loose brick in the surrounding walls.

"The last key was in a window frame. Let's try that," I said, looking back at Maribel.

"This is dumb, Ian. There's no key." She leaned against the wall.

I scanned the perimeter of the wood windows. The rain was rapping against the glass and seeping in around the edges in drops that ran along the cracks in the paint. I wiggled the wood around the frame of each one and looked under the ledge for a hidden key. Nothing. *Maybe Maribel is right,* I thought.

"Did you try the top of the door frame?" Maribel asked me.

"Yeah, but I was too short."

"Lift me up," she said, lifting her arms above her head.

"It's worth a shot," I said. I picked Maribel up in a bear hug and lifted her as high as I could.

"I can't reach anything," she said, struggling. "But I think maybe I can see something!"

I set her back down. "I have an idea. Let's try this." I got on my hands and knees and made my back a table so Maribel could step on me. Her tiptoes dug into my back as she reached up high.

"How's it going up there?" My voice sounded more strained than I intended.

Maribel felt along the top of the frame with her fingertips. "Sorry. It's gross and dusty. There's at least one spider up here, I know it."

I gritted my teeth and tried to hold my back straight as she wiggled around. Dust fell all around me, and I squeezed my eyes shut. *Tink.* I opened my eyes again. A grimy brass key had fallen right between my outstretched fingers.

"Maribel! You did it!"

Maribel hopped off my back. I grabbed the key and stood up. "You did it!" I gave my sister a big hug. "Let's try this thing out, huh!" I dusted the key off against the leg of my jeans and pushed it into the lock. The doorknob turned on the first try. We opened the door and found ourselves in the preserved living area of the keeper's house. We were in the keeper's master bedroom.

Automatic lights flickered on as the door to the hallway shut behind us. My first step into the bedroom was like a step back in time. If it wasn't for the posters and signs labeling the objects in the room, I would have forgotten I was in a museum. The air even smelled the way an old room should smell, sweet and musty like firewood and old books. I looked down at my tennis shoes to find that I'd stepped on a rose petal.

"Mari," I said, holding up the petal. "I think we are in the right place."

"Let's look around!"

I tucked the rose petal into my pocket and sorted through the brass instruments on the desk, careful not to disturb anything. Maribel picked up one of the leather books and started flipping through it. The framed journal page that listed the same symbols from the medallion and First Mate Javenson's journal stood out from the other sketches hanging on the wall to the side of the desk.

I took the medallion out from underneath my T-shirt and turned it over. "Maribel, look, some of the symbols on that page are on the back of this medallion."

"And in the first mate's journal too!" Maribel said, pointing to a series of marks on the pages.

"These symbols here match those!" I said, pulling her journal up next to the framed sketch.

"Ian, those initials are on the bottom of this drawing again. JSJ." Maribel leaned in closer to look at the corner of the framed page.

"Well, that kind of rules out Mayor Juarez, unless he's been alive for like a hundred years," I joked.

"The first mate's real name could be JS Javenson," she suggested.

"Maybe," I said, still looking at the sketch.

"Which of these symbols are on the medallion?" Maribel asked.

"Umm, a frog…a snake with a beard…some zigzag lines…" I rotated the medallion.

"That's not very helpful. Read the names the book gives them. I'll match them that way." Maribel held her pointer finger to the captain's journal, ready to search for the symbols.

"Okay, uh, there's *mica. Muyhica. Cuhupqua. Aca.* then there's *ubchihica*," I answered, matching the symbols on the medallion to the ones from the framed page.

"Okay, the captain's journal says that those words mean to look for with open eyes, the darkness grows with closed eyes…ears covered, deafness…connected, resolved?…what's the last one?"

"*Ubchihica*," I said.

"Okay, that says, paint the shining moon."

"Maribel, that makes no sense."

"Well, I'm not an expert in hieroglyphics or whatever this is! I'm just telling you what the journal says!"

"Okay, 'to look for with open eyes'…then what?"

"Read the symbol names again," Maribel said.

"*Mica, muyhica, cuhupqua, aca, ubchihica*—oh my gosh!" I jumped back, almost dropping the medallion. The snake symbol slithered around the whole medallion and back into place. All of the symbols glowed a deep red, and a shock wave pulsed through my fingers.

"What is it?" Maribel asked.

"The medallion! It electrocuted me!" I turned it over and took in a sharp breath. The deep red glow was shining out of the emerald eyes now, like two hot coals. The whole medallion was letting out a low, almost electric buzz.

Maribel touched the glowing emerald with the tip of her finger. "Ouch!" She jumped back.

"I told you."

"What do we do?" Maribel shook her hand from the shock.

"What do you mean 'what do we do'? We put it back and get out of here!"

"We can't put it back *now*. It's bright red and lighting up! Don't you think they'll notice?"

I took a few steps backward from the desk, still staring at the framed journal sketch that JSJ had written. "Who cares if they notice? It's not our problem!"

But as I backed up, a huge shadow fell over me. The air took on a smell of sweat, sea salt, and blueberry muffins. I turned around to see Malachi staring down at me with an even bigger frown than he'd had the last time I'd seen him. A squeak of terror escaped Maribel, and she rushed to my side, holding onto my arm with both hands and hiding behind me.

"What have you done?" he growled.

"I-I..." I didn't know what to say.

Malachi's disgruntled glare went from the glowing medallion to me and then transformed into a scowl as he looked past me. He stomped toward the window, almost in sync with the thunder. *Boom boom boom.* Everything in the room shook with each step. Even the brass instruments rattled on the little table. With Malachi distracted by the window, Maribel and I inched backward slowly, ready to escape.

Maribel tucked the journal inside her jacket. *Cree-eak.* The floorboards whined.

"It's not me you'll wanna be running from," Malachi said without turning around. "They're coming for us. I don't know what you did, but you've called them and they're headed right toward us."

I couldn't see past Malachi's massive frame to the window. Couldn't see what he was looking at. "Who? Who's coming for us?"

Malachi turned around slowly and spoke evenly as he looked at Maribel and me. "Captain Larsen and his cursed crew. The ghosts from the *Olivia*."

"I've seen them before. They don't do anything but float around on the water singing sea shanties." I let the glowing medallion fall back on my chest, this time on top of my T-shirt.

"Oh, they do a lot more than that. Especially now," Malachi mumbled, stomping past us toward the hall. "You'd better come with me."

Chapter 13

The Curse

We followed Malachi as he huffed and lumbered through the keeper's house and toward the treasure room. My tennis shoes squeaked against the wood planks along the way, smudging the dust. Even though Malachi's steps looked heavy, his boots didn't leave any footprints.

"So, you've seen the crew before," he said over his shoulder. "That means you know about the curse?"

"The curse?" Maribel asked.

"That'd be a no then," Malachi said, stopping again to stare down at both of us. The red glow of the medallion washed over his face, casting shadows across his mouth and eyes, making him look even scarier. "The crew of the *Olivia* sailed out over a hundred years ago. Explorers in search of El Dorado. Well, they found it. Came back with a boat full of treasure. Gold from South America. Never made it to shore with their gold, though. Their boat hit a rough patch out in the bay during a storm, and the rescue ships the keepers sent out…couldn't save them. All they could do was salvage some of the treasure and—"

"And First Mate Javenson's journal?" Maribel asked.

"How did you know about that?" Malachi snapped.

I tried to stop Maribel from showing him, but she pulled the journal out of her jacket anyway. "We found it in the lighthouse."

Malachi reached for it, but I pulled Maribel back. "So, the sailors from the *Olivia* drowned, and the rescue boats couldn't save them. That's sad, but not strange. What's the curse?"

"*Haaa ha ha.*" A cold empty laugh rattled the colossal sailor. "Well, you've seen it! The unhappy souls from the *Olivia* wander the sea in Castillo Bay, cursed by the South American gold to live on as ghosts forever. The wreck was a curse, too. I'm a sea dog. I've been out there. Ain't no rocks or nothing should have caused their boat to go under. But any vessel that crosses the shadow of the sea where their ship went down finds themselves in trouble too."

"In trouble?" I asked.

"Ever since the *Olivia* went down out there, any ship that crosses it goes down too. Little fishing boats, speed boats, a ferry full of football players in the forties. Anyone who's gone out diving in search of the wreckage from that or any other boat has never come back. The restless ghosts from the *Olivia* just pull them down to the depths to join them in their eternal despair." Malachi shook his head and scratched at his scraggly beard.

I thought of the divers I'd seen on the shore when I had ice cream with Maribel and Dad. The sock hop ghosts. They must have been a teenage couple just out on the sea. The sailors from the football game. The football players. *Did they all go down sailing over the wreckage of the Olivia?* I imagined the crew walking across the waves and chanting their creepy song.

"But they stay on the ocean, right?" I asked.

"Well, they usually do, but they're headed toward us right now. Who's to stop them from dragging everyone in Castillo Bay back into the ocean to join them in the watery grave they guard?"

"That won't happen," I said decisively. "We won't let it. Why haven't you found a way to put a stop to the curse if you've known about it all this time? You really just watched as boat after boat of people drowned in the same spot?"

"Well, it ain't my problem, is it?" Malachi shouted. "People oughtta know better than sailing out where it ain't safe. The sea is dangerous! People shouldn't take a boat out there if they can't handle it! Just like they shouldn't walk around with an ancient medallion and go turning it on and makin' it glow and whatnot! You know what? Why don't you pipe down and give me that journal—"

Malachi made a move toward Maribel, and I stepped between them. "I think she should hang onto it for now. Where are you leading us?" I sounded braver than I felt.

Malachi stepped back, out of the red light from the medallion. He narrowed his eyes as he turned around and started walking again. "We're going to the treasure room."

"Good," I said. "Let's put the medallion back where it belongs and break the curse."

Malachi's heavy shoulders shook with an empty chuckle. "Little late for that, don't you think, pipsqueak?"

The uncomfortable feeling in my stomach returned when I caught a glimpse of Maribel's face. We were much more involved in this than I'd hoped we would be.

We entered the treasure room, and the lights

flickered on, revealing walls full of pictures, artifacts, and displays. It was so bright and pristine compared to the rustic warmth of the rest of the keeper's house.

"Wait here," Malachi barked as he walked to the end of the room toward a glass door that said Employees Only.

Maribel and I obeyed, feeling that we had no other option. I walked over to look at the display wall of historical photos, where I caught a glimpse of some of the pictures I'd seen when I was researching the medallion online. The first showed Captain Larsen standing near the hull of the *Olivia*, a family of keepers by the house in the early twenties. I took a step closer to look at one of the pictures of the keeper's family, blinked my eyes hard, and looked again. It was a black-and-white photo. Standing in front of the keeper's house with one arm around a woman who held the hand of a toddler and the other around a kid about Maribel's age, was Stanley Jones. It was unmistakable. He was the exact likeness of the man I'd talked to during the football game. The man who had been calmly raking the yard in a storm. The man who snuck into the tower with an armful of roses. Impossible. That would mean he was over a hundred years old. Over a hundred years old without aging a day?

"Maribel," I whispered. But my sister couldn't hear me. A whisper wasn't loud enough, especially with the steady patter of rain on the roof above us.

"Maribel," I said a little louder. She still didn't turn around.

I turned back to the picture and read the gallery tag. "*Castillo Bay Lighthouse Keeper Family. Jeremiah Jones with wife Sarah, son Thomas, and daughter Elizabeth. Jeremiah, Sarah, and Thomas all tragically passed in 1922 during the hurricane that capsized the Olivia.*" I took a step back, disappointed. I could have sworn that the man was Stanley. The photo looked like him down to the bow tie, the eyes, the gentle smile. The woman had a rose tucked into her hair behind her ear and the little boy held a toy boat. My eyes adjusted from the photo to the glass in front of it where my own reflection stared back at me. Tired eyes and a serious expression. I almost didn't recognize myself. The normally green stone eyes of the medallion were glowing red. Pulling me in, even through the reflection. A whisper rang in my ears. A chant. Drums. The red eyes pulsed along with the rhythm. Growing louder.

"Welcome back, Ian." I jumped when I heard a woman's voice carry across the clean room and turned around to see Miss Jones standing next to Malachi outside the glass door that was swinging shut.

"Miss Jones, I—"

"Malachi tells me you have something for me," she said calmly. Was there an undercurrent of irritation? *Is she mad at me?*

Maribel left the artifacts on the wall near the entrance of the treasure room she'd been studying and came to join me, holding my hand. I took a deep breath in. *Time to come clean,* I thought.

"We are here to return the medallion," I said. "I'm really sorry that I have it, and that I haven't given it back sooner. I didn't take it on purpose. I—"

"How did you make it glow?" Miss Jones interrupted, stepping toward me to lift the medallion from my chest with two fingers. She let it rest there, looking at the glowing emerald eyes as if the medallion had the same effect on her that it had on me. Like it was hypnotizing her.

"We said the words from the back," Maribel said. "We were trying to figure out what it meant, and when Ian said the words out loud, the snake marking slithered around it and then it started to glow. And it shocked our fingers when it woke up."

I looked at Maribel, impressed. I hadn't even put together the fact that saying the words from the symbols had caused the medallion to start glowing, but it made sense. I was so busy being annoyed with my sister most of the time that I didn't always take the time to recognize that she could actually be pretty clever.

"Is that so?" Miss Jones asked, still studying the medallion.

"We don't have time for this," Malachi growled. "Captain Larsen and his crew are threatening to come ashore. I saw them with my own eyes out the window."

"They're always a threat," Miss Jones answered, dropping the medallion and letting it fall back against my chest. "That's the problem."

"You can see the ghosts too?" I asked.

"Anyone who has touched the medallion can see the ghosts," Miss Jones said matter-of-factly. "That's how I knew you had it when you told Mrs. Rodriguez you'd seen our friend Malachi." She looked down at me with a sly smile, as if we were both in on a secret. I gaped at Malachi and back at Miss Jones.

"Malachi's a ghost?"

"I'm afraid so."

My jaw dropped.

"I knew it," Mari whispered.

"And you knew I had the medallion?"

Miss Jones nodded. "Didn't even have to watch the

video."

"Why didn't you say anything? When you came to the booth?"

"I was planning to, but then I could tell you were a good kid. I trusted that you would find a way to make it right."

Miss Jones trusted me? She knew I had the necklace and she didn't call me out?

"I didn't take it on purpose," I said. "My friends were messing around, and they put it in my bag to play a trick on me."

Mrs. Jones clicked her tongue. "Those don't sound like great friends." She pulled her phone from her pocket to send a quick message.

"They're not. They're the worst." Mari agreed.

"I'm starting to figure that out."

I took a moment to let that sink in. *Anyone who has touched the medallion can see the ghosts.* I'd started seeing ghosts after I tried to keep the medallion from falling. JC and Marcos would have touched the medallion when they put it in my backpack.

That's why they could see the ghost crew when other people couldn't. *Who else has touched it?* I asked myself.

The glass door opened, and Miss Ortiz stepped out, carrying a coffee tumbler and dropping her cell phone into her blazer pocket. The *click click click* of her heels on the crisp tile rang out across the room. "Ian from the bakery booth?" she said, smirking at me.

"*Hola*, Miss Ortiz." I knew I was blushing.

"Let's have a look at that medallion, shall we?" She untucked a pair of glasses from the front collar of her shirt, unfolded them, and put them on.

I lifted the medallion from my neck and gave it to her, taking a deep breath and feeling like an elephant had just rolled off my chest.

Miss Ortiz handed me her coffee tumbler to hold so that she could inspect the medallion in her fingers, turning it over to study the symbols on the back. "Let's examine this in your office," she said to Miss Jones. They moved toward the glass door.

Maribel skipped up to join them. "I have a list here that translates the symbols!" she said, eager to join the two women.

I hung back, gripping Miss Ortiz's warm coffee tumbler awkwardly.

The ladies exchanged small smiles above Maribel's head, and Miss Jones pulled the door open.

"Follow me then!" Miss Ortiz said to Maribel. "And what's your name…"

I could hear them talking down the hallway through the glass door as I stood frozen to the spot in the middle of the treasure room, the red glow disappearing along with their fading voices.

I looked back at Malachi, whose face was set in a grimace.

"Coming, Ian?" Miss Jones said pleasantly, still holding the door.

I guess we aren't done with this after all, I thought. But how could I be rude to the woman who'd just been so nice to me, even though I'd been hiding her priceless stolen treasure? This woman who trusted me.

I took a deep breath and followed Miss Jones to her office.

Chapter 14

The Sun and the Moon

"Wow, I hope I have an office this cool when I grow up," Maribel said as we entered the big room Miss Jones led us to.

Shelves full of every size and color of books, framed maritime maps, and diagrams of different kinds of ships lined the walls. Ships in bottles, masks from Africa, and clay pots wove in and around the books.

"Thank you." Miss Jones closed the laptop on her corner desk and pulled in scattered ceramic mugs with various ocean puns or pictures of turtles or sailboats.

"Is that you in Egypt?" Maribel marveled at a photo of Miss Jones on a camel in front of the pyramids. The one next to it showed her in full diving gear on a big boat somewhere with a row of other divers squinting in the sun.

"Yes," she said, dusting crumbs into a trash can under her desk. "That camel nearly ate my shoe!"

Maribel looked to me to sign it for her, because Miss Jones had turned her head away and mumbled a little while she was cleaning her desk. I couldn't remember the hand sign for camel, so I hesitated before finally spelling it out.

"I'm sorry," Miss Jones said, eyeing the interaction. "Should I—"

"It's okay," I said. "Maribel just has trouble hearing if it is loud, or if she can't read your lips. It's great if you know sign language, but it's okay if you don't. A lot of people don't."

"I'll try to speak more clearly and be thoughtful of that." Miss Jones reshuffled a stack of papers on another corner of her desk. They were the scavenger hunts she'd made for us along with a bag full of the coins she'd given the winners on our field trip. I reached into my jeans pocket instinctively. My coin was still there, along with the two keys we'd found.

Miss Ortiz took a seat at one of the four chairs around a table across from the desk near an open computer, a fancy zip-up notebook, and a leather laptop bag. Behind the table, a big printed poster with pictures of round stones that had symbols carved into them like the ones on the back of the medallion took up most of the wall space. A list of symbols with their meanings written beside them was scribbled down the side of the poster. It looked like Miss Jones had gone in with pencil and added some things to the chart, like months of the calendar year and words about the meanings. Next to the poster of symbols, a map of Castillo Bay was pinned to the wall with thumbtacks. She had circled an area in the middle of the water with a red felt pen, and drawn some red x's by the shore.

"Is this the area where the *Olivia* went down?" I asked, pointing to the map as the others took a seat around the table by Miss Jones's desk.

"I believe so," Miss Jones said, pulling out a chair for Malachi and then rolling the chair from her desk around to the table too. "But no one knows for sure. I've set up markers out in the bay where I think it is so that people don't sail through it. People believe there are dangerous rocks there."

I nodded and pulled up a chair to sit at the table with Miss Ortiz, Miss Jones, Maribel, and Malachi.

Miss Ortiz was turning the medallion over in her hands carefully and examining the symbols, making notes in her fancy notebook. "Well, a few things about this medallion. It is from Colombia. There's no doubt about that. The emeralds here are iconic of Colombia. We're famous for them. The zoomorphic symbols, that is, symbols that look like animals, on the back and around the border, are definitely Muisca. I would need to get it back to my lab for carbon dating, but I believe it is at least a thousand years old."

"Is this the medallion from the legends?" I asked.

Miss Ortiz looked up at me with a smile. "You know of the legend of the medallion? Tell me."

I rubbed at the back of my neck. "Just that there was a sun god, and he gave immortality to two people, kind of like God making Adam from dirt and—"

"Tena and Fura," Miss Ortiz nodded. "The sun god and moon goddess were said to have given this medallion to them to grant them immortality. It is less a creation story and more a story about how worthy those two were to receive this gift."

"But they lost it," I said. "Fura lied to Tena and betrayed him when she kissed one of the Spanish explorers and they lost their immortality, right?"

"Something like that." Miss Ortiz pulled a magnifying glass from her bag and studied the emeralds on the medallion. "It is said that their rage over the deception caused disharmony. The gods took away their immortality along with Tena's ability to hear Fura's apology. Eventually, Tena died fighting the explorers who would inevitably steal all of the treasures that they could from Colombia. This medallion, though, was carried by the Zipa and placed in a sacred temple where the moon could shine on it during important phases of the lunar cycle."

"Because of the moonbeam from the legend?" I asked.

Miss Ortiz nodded.

"You believe this is the medallion from that legend?" Miss Jones asked.

"It's possible."

"How did it get here, though?" Maribel asked.

Miss Ortiz took a sip of her coffee and sat back in her chair. "It was taken when the temple was raided in the 1920s. A flood of explorers looking for immortality and gold came to Colombia and other countries in South America. They plundered our temples, drained our lakes, and dug up the earth, looking for anything they could find. After they'd taken all they could, they left. Left our broken temples and gaping graves with boatfuls of our treasure, never looking back."

Miss Jones placed a hand on Miss Ortiz's arm. "I'm sorry."

"But we're doing what we can to make it right, aren't we?" I asked hopefully.

"Yes, some are," Miss Ortiz said, sitting forward and picking up the medallion. "And you were right to call me, Desiree. This artifact is an important part of Colombian history."

Malachi reached up to twist at his beard.

Miss Ortiz set the medallion back down on the table. "*Dios mio*, I can feel the fury coursing through it just by touching it. Some say this medallion can grant immortality, but it also carries with it the rage Tena felt from being lied to. The rage that caused him to kill every man who stepped across his borders. The rage that eventually killed him, too."

"Grant immortality? How? That's impossible." Even as I said it, the glowing medallion pulled me in and I had to look away.

"It is possible. It's just not the immortality you think it is. Not what you see in the adventure movies." A new voice joined us. I turned around to see Stanley Jones leaning on the door frame. "Hello again, Ian." He winked at me.

"Grampa!" Miss Jones hopped up from her seat. She glanced back at me and Maribel nervously.

"Grampa?" I asked. Stanley barely looked old enough to be someone's dad.

"Actually, this is my great-grandfather, but I've always just called him Grampa." She turned back to Stanley. "What are you doing here?"

Stanley's eyes were locked on the glowing medallion. "That thing called me here. I think the crew of the *Olivia* must have gotten the message too because Captain Larsen just paid me a visit out in the yard. He hasn't been on shore for years."

"What did he say?" Malachi leaned forward quickly.

"Nothing to get your long johns in a bunch about, Malachi." Stanley went to the table to sit in the seat Miss Jones offered him. "Said he could feel 'unbridled rage surging in the sea' or something like that…and informed me that he'd be back at dusk with his crew and that we'd better give him the medallion or they'd 'give in to the rage' and start causing trouble for everyone in Castillo

Bay, dead or alive."

Stanley winked at me.

"Well, that does seem like something to get your long johns in a bunch about, doesn't it?" Miss Ortiz took another sip of her coffee.

"They want more than just the medallion. They want—"

"It doesn't matter what they want. We've just gotta figure out how to get things back to normal and put the medallion back on display where it's always been," Stanley said matter-of-factly. "Then that crew can turn around and march right back to the depths of the ocean where they belong."

"You think it'll be that simple?" Stanley and Malachi stared at one another across the table.

Everyone sat in silence at the table, lost in thought, watching the pulsing red glow of the medallion. *Ding.* We all jumped at the sound of my phone alerting me.

"Sorry," I said, scrambling forward and reaching into my back pocket. "It's my mom."

"Oh, you know what," Miss Jones said, checking her watch. "It's almost two. They'll be letting tours back in shortly."

I looked at my phone, expecting to see a text from Mom. Instead, it was a message from my dad.

—*Hey kiddo, 'sup? Made it to the festival after all, if you two want to meet up before I have to go back to work.*—

I stared at the phone for a minute. Mad. I didn't know why. Maybe it was the anger surging through the air from the medallion that Miss Ortiz was talking about. I tucked my phone back in my pocket without looking at Maribel, even though I knew she was looking at me, curious about what the text had said.

"Let's meet up again at dusk," Miss Jones suggested. "We can form a plan then."

"That will give me time to do some research," Miss Ortiz said.

"Will you be joining us, Ian?" Stanley looked at me with a twinkle in his eye.

"Well, sir…I…" I looked down at the table.

"Seems to me that you and your sister bring something special to this whole operation. This medallion has been in our possession for something like a hundred years, and nobody has brought it to life before you two. I think, if you're up for it, you two might just be the key to helping us break the curse and banish these pirates." Stanley smiled the slow, gentle smile he'd shown me in the yard the night before.

"Don't be absurd, they're kids! And they don't know anything about the curse. Neither do you! We don't need to do anything but get Larsen off our tail." Malachi and Stanley glared at one another with a hostility that seemed it had been brewing for longer than I'd been alive.

"Ian, Maribel, you can join us if you want to. I feel like a horrible grown-up asking kids to get involved with something like this," Miss Jones said.

I looked over at Maribel, and she nodded. "We're already involved. We'll be here."

"What will you do with the medallion?" Malachi asked.

"We can't put the medallion back on display, not with it glowing the way it is. We can keep it locked up here in my office." Miss Jones walked over to her desk and pulled out one of the drawers. She wrapped the medallion in a cloth and placed it gently in the drawer before closing it and locking it.

Even through the metal desk drawer, the pulse of the glowing medallion pulled me in, and I knew it was going to take more than a little lock and key to keep those ghost pirates from getting to it.

Chapter 15

The Festival

"So what do we do?" Maribel asked when we'd stepped out of the crisp white museum and into the grey air still damp from the storm. The clouds overhead drifted by in cracked sections, like the broken bricks from the lighthouse tower walls, and the sun crumbled through in brief slivers that shimmered, then passed on.

"I think we should study that journal some more and meet back with them at seven, but we say that we need some answers before we help them," I said.

"But what about Mom? She's worried about us. She's waiting for us!" Maribel bit her lip.

"We'll have to find some excuse," I said. "I don't like the thought of hurting Mom's feelings either, but if we let Captain Larsen and his crew come ashore, they'll hurt everyone, including Mom. We have to do this."

"Okay," Maribel said. "What did she say when she texted you?" A slice of sunshine danced across her face, reminding me of a crescent moon.

"Actually, it was Dad."

"Dad?" She took a step back, clouds and shadows returning.

"I guess he got off work early or something, and he was asking if we want to hang out with him for a bit." I tucked my hands in my pockets and fiddled with the coin and keys. *Why didn't I tell everyone at the table about these?* I asked myself.

"I don't want to," Maribel said firmly.

I wasn't sure whether I wanted to meet up with Dad, but hearing Maribel say that she didn't made me mad. "Why not? We hardly get to see him! If he wants to buy us ice cream or whatever, let's just do it."

"All he wants to do is buy us ice cream, Ian. We're never going to get to do more than that," Maribel signed. "I heard him and Mom fighting the other night and—"

"What are you talking about?" I signed back. "You love hanging out with Dad. You two are always like 'giggle giggle' and 'oh princess, you're amazing' and all that. And anyway, I don't know how we could tell him no. He'd be upset!"

"I'm not his favorite. I'm the reason they got a divorce. I was too much for him to handle." Maribel's eyes were glistening with tears. "Don't you think I've noticed that he never bothered to learn sign language? Even a little?"

I didn't know what to say. I guess Maribel and I never talked much about how she felt about things. I thought she was fine.

"I heard him and Mom talking the other night," Maribel said. "They thought they were being quiet. I know they thought I wouldn't be able to hear them, but I did. Mom said, 'It's fine that you quit on me, but don't quit on your children.' I don't know what that means. What does it mean, Ian?" Maribel was yelling now. She looked up at me with tears streaming down her face.

I found a bench for us to sit down on, and I put my arm around my sister.

"Maribel, you aren't too much for anyone. Dad left

because…because…" I remembered what I'd seen out my window last year before one of Mom and Dad's fights. Before they sat us down at the kitchen table. The lady in the front seat of Dad's car with the blond hair. The way that she pulled him in. The way another lady pulled my dad's face to hers to kiss him on the mouth before he walked up the sidewalk to our front door…the night that my parents had their biggest fight ever. When they were still married. Before everything fell apart. I tried to block it from my memory and go on. "Because sometimes grown-ups have fights that don't make sense to us. But it isn't your fault. It isn't my fault either. Dad loves you."

Maribel sat quietly for a moment, looking down at the damp grass. "Okay, but you better text Mom and let her know, so she doesn't worry. She worries about us all the time, you know."

I shrugged and took my phone from my pocket. I sent Mom a message letting her know we would hang out with Dad for a while, and Dad a message asking where he wanted to meet us.

On our way to find Dad, we bumped into the two kids who were in the running for the World's Worst Friends award—JC and Marcos.

"Hey, Ian!" Marcos shouted, waving his hot dog at me and elbowing JC to let him know I was there.

"Ian! We've been looking for you, man! Whatever happened to the…" JC shot a sideward glance at my sister. "*You know…*"

"Wouldn't you like to know!" Maribel shouted defiantly, standing between us with her hands on her hips. "Maybe if you didn't run off like a couple of scaredy-cat babies—"

"We're not babies! You're the little baby," JC said to my sister before turning to me. "Dude, get your sister under control!"

A few kids my age were looking at us now.

"For real, Ian. Ditch your annoying little baby sister and come hang out with us. Then you can tell us everything," Marcos said, taking a big bite out of his hot dog and scowling at Maribel.

Maribel turned back to look at me with wide, hopeful eyes. I wanted to tell her to run back to Mom. I wanted to forget all about the medallion and the whole mess and just spend a day at the festival with my friends. Maybe pretend like none of it ever happened.

But then I thought about the way Maribel followed me up the rickety metal stairs of the crumbling lighthouse. How she took my hand and said we were in this together, even though she didn't have to. My sister was loyal. My sister was brave. My sister was my real friend.

"Maribel is right," I said, sounding stronger than I felt. "You guys are a couple of scared babies. You just ditched me out there when I needed you."

"We didn't ditch you! Right, Marcos? We were gonna go up there, but then we knew we had to go back or we'd get in trouble, that's all. I thought you were with us," JC said.

"Yeah, swear to God! We thought you were running with us! We didn't know why you stayed back!" Marcos added.

"No, you didn't," I said, shaking my head. "You ditched me because you were scared. You ditched me because that's what you do. You guys think you're so funny or you're so smart. You're not. You know Maribel climbed the lighthouse tower with me? Know she was the one brave enough to go with me to the keeper's house? Not you. Maribel."

A slow smile spread across my sister's face.

"Whatever. We didn't want to hang out with you anyway. You're always so boring."

"I'd rather be boring than be your friend, JC," I said matter-of-factly.

Marcos's mouth fell open, and half of his hot dog rolled out. JC clenched both of his fists as redness rose in his cheeks. People didn't stand up to him very often.

"Come on, Maribel," I said, holding out my hand for my sister.

JC was about to say something, but Maribel beat him to it.

"I talked to the pirate ghosts," she whispered as we walked past. "They're coming for you, JC. They're coming for both of you. Tonight."

JC and Marcos staggered back. Marcos dropped his hot dog completely and reached out for us as we walked away.

"Liar!" JC yelled. "Liar!"

"I don't wanna mess with pirate ghosts!" Marcos cried. "Ian, take me with you! Maribel, take me with you guys!"

JC pulled him back by the collar, and they started squabbling. I chuckled as we walked away. JC and Marcos continued to fight with each other in screechy, panicked voices.

"That was a nice touch," I said to my sister. "I think you made them pee their pants back there."

"Nobody messes with my brother," Maribel answered, beaming.

We found my dad at the carnival games, throwing balls to knock down ducks for prizes. How long had he been there?

He greeted us with a quick smile as he continued throwing. "Hey, kiddos! One of y'all got ten bucks? I hit five more, and we can get the big prize."

I dug in my pocket and gave him some of the money Mom had given me for working in the booth with her. *I thought he said he had a bunch of extra money.*

"Thanks, bud." He handed it to the high school kid running the carnival game. The guy rolled his eyes and handed Dad five more balls.

We watched him hit duck after duck until he was done. My dad was pretty athletic. He was always telling us how he was the star of whatever team he played on, whether it was football, baseball, or anything really.

"All right!" he shouted after knocking the last one down. "Which one do you want, Maribel?" He pointed to the row of stuffed animals at the top, the biggest prizes.

"I'm okay," she said awkwardly.

"Oh, come on. You still like puppies?"

Maribel looked at me, confused. The noise from the carnival was too much. I signed to her that he'd asked if she wanted a stuffed puppy doll, and she looked back at Dad and nodded. *Why is she acting so strange,* I thought. *She's normally so bubbly with Dad.* In fact, I usually found it annoying how she was always kissing up to him, but not today.

Dad didn't notice the difference. Just as he pulled down the dog to hand it to Maribel, a squealing woman jumped between us and took hold of the stuffed animal. "I love it, thank you, baby!"

I staggered back, overwhelmed by a sea of blonde hair and flowery perfume. Mari's eyes watered a little as she dropped the hands she'd been holding up, waiting to receive the prize.

"Ashlee, what are you doing?" Dad's eyes shifted from each of us to the woman squeezing Mari's stuffed animal.

She turned around and took my dad's arm with one hand, suffocating the prize puppy doll in the other. "I didn't wanna stay back with our friends. I want a night out with my man!"

It was like I was back in my bedroom with the curtain pulled back, looking out at the street. I hadn't wanted to believe that my dad would let some lady in his car that wasn't Mom. Would kiss some lady that wasn't Mom. Why did I believe my dad when he told me I'd been seeing things?

The woman fluttered thick eyelashes at my dad and then turned to flash a big, charming smile at me that made the tips of my ears burn. "Hi, Ian," she said. They were the same eyelashes that made Marcos drool at school. The same smile she used to greet all the kids in the hallway. It was Miss Ashlee, the teacher's aide, and she was clutching my dad's arm like he was going to save her from drowning.

Instinctively, I took Maribel's hand. It was shaking. I thought of a thousand things to say. A thousand things to ask. I looked at my dad, waiting for him to say something. Anything. Waiting for him to apologize for leaving me out in the dark about this big secret he'd been keeping.

My dad held my gaze for a moment, then looked away.

"I'm glad your mom is *finally* letting us hang out."
Miss Ashlee ran her tongue over her teeth, red glossed
lips reflecting the harsh sun peeking through the clouds.
"What do we wanna do next? Cotton candy?"

Maribel was looking up at me. Waiting for answers.
I didn't have time to sign everything for her, or maybe I
just didn't know the best way to tell her.

"It's Mom who doesn't let us come over then, huh?"
I asked, realizing that I wasn't the only one in the dark.

"Well, of course! Your dad is always so sad that she
won't let you stay at the house with us!" Miss Ashlee
smiled at me genuinely.

I looked back at Dad, who seemed occupied with
something over my shoulder. Red lipstick smeared all
over his face. I wanted to punch him.

"Right. Well, it's too bad we can't hang out tonight
either. Mom needs us back at the booth," I lied.

"Oh." Miss Ashlee flipped her hair. "Well, maybe
next time, right, Blakey?"

Dad looked back at us and smiled. "Maybe next
time."

"Miss Ashlee," I said, looking right at her. "That
dog you have there. That's my sister's."

Miss Ashlee pouted and held it a little tighter, but I
didn't budge.

"Give me the doll, please," I said without blinking.

She rolled her eyes and held out the doll by the ear.

"Thanks," I said, taking the stuffed animal and
handing it to my sister. "See ya around."

I waited for my dad to ask us to stay. To tell Miss
Ashlee that he needed time to talk to us. But I didn't have
to wait long. They skipped off together toward the
carnival games, and I was grateful that Maribel couldn't

hear my dad tell Miss Ashlee he'd win her another doll.

Maribel and I stood together without talking for what seemed like hours but must have only been half a minute, with the stupid carnival music rattling my eardrums and the bright lights from the flashy games swirling all around us. I clenched and unclenched my fists, trying to decide what to say to my sister. When I turned to look at Mari, I saw that she understood enough already. There were tears in her eyes.

Maribel squeezed the stuffed puppy with her little hands and threw it down into the dirt.

Chapter 16

Fight with Mom

I knew it didn't make sense, but I was really mad at my mom. She knew all this time that Dad had a house with a girlfriend living in it, and she never said anything. She let us think he was trying to be a better dad for us. Let us think we weren't good enough, and that's why he left. Just stood there silently nodding all the time while he told us lies, or when we repeated those lies to her like they were true. I didn't understand why everyone treated me like I was stupid. On our way to Mom's booth, I felt my insides boiling up so much I thought I might explode.

Mom caught us coming toward her and waved. Her warm ignorant smile made me feel even more frustrated.

"Dad isn't working?" I blurted. "Dad and Miss Ashlee...are they married? They have a house! He's here with her instead of us—"

My mother's face fell, losing all of its color. She looked more like a ghost than Captain Larsen. "How did you? Listen, I—"

"Listen to what? You've been lying to us all this time!"

She was a deer in headlights. "Come inside the tent, sit down. Let's talk about everything."

I gritted my teeth and stomped into the tent, Maribel following tentatively behind me.

Mom pulled out a chair and handed me a cookie, but I pushed it away.

"I don't want a cookie. I want to know what is going on. Why did Miss Ashlee say that you won't let us see them? I didn't even know that—"

Color returned to her face then. Red. "They said that I won't—? Okay, let's start from the beginning. Your father is dating Miss Ashlee from your school. They live in a house they bought a few months ago. They have been together for some time. Since…well, it doesn't matter. I haven't been keeping you from them, honey. Your father didn't want you to know."

"So you lied for him?"

Mom was speechless. She sat on the ground beside me and placed one hand on my leg and the other on Maribel's. Bells and clicking boots and children laughing at carnival games all swirled around me as we sat under the red pop-up tent. I stared up at the white metal frame, rusted at the joints.

"I'm sorry. I know this is hard. I just haven't been able to bring myself to talk to you about it."

"So he has a house? It isn't too small for us?"

Mom nodded slowly.

Maribel signed, "You didn't kick him out, did you? He left."

Mom shrugged her shoulders. "It's complicated." She signed back.

I thought of the way that Mrs. Rodriguez had looked at me every time Miss Ashlee came into our class to drop off papers. Other teachers acted weird around me too sometimes.

"Does everyone know? Everyone but us?"

"I don't know," Mom said. "I don't know who

knows. I try not to spend too much time thinking about it. Ian, your dad loves you—"

"I don't care. All this time I thought Dad left because I wasn't good enough at sports, and Mari thought it was because he didn't want to learn sign language."

Mom's forehead furrowed. "Kids, no. I'm so sorry. No, it isn't your fault at all." She looked back and forth from me to Maribel, tears in her eyes. "Kids, you're perfect. There's nothing you did that made your father leave and nothing you could have done to make him stay."

Hot tears burned at my lower eyelids. "It doesn't feel good to be lied to."

"I know. I'm sorry. I was trying to protect you."

"But you didn't protect us, Mom. You protected Dad's lie." I wiped at my eyes with my sleeve.

Mom shrank back as if she'd been wounded. "I'm sorry," she said again.

But I didn't really hear her. Why did everyone treat me like I was stupid?

Maribel sat on the grass beside Mom and hugged her. Kissing up, as usual. Mom stroked Mari's hair and looked up at me hopefully. I folded my arms and looked away. How could she lie to me like that? She's always talking about how important it is to be honest and how lies are like poison. And she was right. Lies had destroyed my family. As I was looking away from my mom, I thought of the story of Fura and Tena and how their lies caused the end of their entire civilization.

I looked back at Mom and Maribel, the way they were hugging. I wanted to hug Mom too, but I just couldn't.

"I need to walk around for a while," I said.

Mom bit her lip. "I understand."

Maribel took hold of Mom's hand. "I'm going to stay with Mom."

I shrugged my shoulders. "Fine."

Mom stood up too and kissed my forehead. I fought the instinct to pull away. "Keep your phone on you. If you want to watch the fireworks with me, I'll save you a seat."

Her weak, hopeful smile made me sick to my stomach. I just shrugged again and stepped out into the carnival.

I wanted to clear my head, but all the noise and the bustling of the crowd just amplified my thoughts. I didn't understand anything that was going on with my parents. I didn't understand why the medallion had ended up in my backpack or why a crew of ghost pirates was my problem now. My stomach gnawed and clawed at me. I wished I'd accepted that cookie from my mom.

I pushed through a bunch of people waiting in line to throw darts at a balloon and stood in the crowd of people watching cow patty bingo, where people stand around a cow pen and wait to see if it uses the restroom on one of the squares somebody marked out in chalk. All the spectators stood holding the tickets they'd bought marked with square numbers, and the cow walked around her pen on top of chalk squares that matched up to the ticket numbers. If the cow peed on a square, they'd get twenty bucks and if she laid a patty, they'd get a hundred.

It was a big brown Hereford cow named Teriyaki. Everybody was tightly gripping their tickets, bumping into each other and jumping up and down as Teriyaki raised her tail up between two squares. I backed up and let the people rush in, taking the wad of cash out of my pocket to see if I had enough money left for lunch. Four dollars. There was a hamburger truck across the way, ironically within sight of the cow. I didn't have enough money for a burger, which is what I really wanted, but I figured maybe I could get some fries.

I kicked a rock along the brick street to the burger truck, mad at my dad, mad at my mom, mad at Marcos and JC, mad at Mari for staying with mom, mad at my four dollars. I stood in line and bit my lower lip until it was almost bleeding, trying hard not to cry. Would this whole place be swarming with ghosts by nightfall? Was it all my fault if they were?

I jumped when I felt a strong hand grip my shoulder and turned around to see Grandad standing beside me. I opened my mouth to speak but had nothing to say.

Grandad just drew me in for a hug and patted my back. "I'm glad to find you here," he said. "Are you hungry?"

Grandad and I sat on a curb eating our burgers and fries, watching the crowd close in around cow patty bingo, everyone hoping for something from the cow. It had been a false alarm before, and all the squares under the cow were still clean. Grandad told me that was the fun part about cow patty bingo. People spent all day thinking the cow was about to do something. He said he'd seen people try to sneak prunes to the cows through the fences before.

"Your mom called me. Told me you've had a rough day." Grandad offered me a ketchup packet for my fries.

"I don't want to talk about it," I said.

"No one wants to talk about these things," Grandad

answered. "But isn't that why you're mad, *mijo*? Because no one talked to you about it?"

I stacked my fries carefully in little houses around my ketchup. "I guess so. I just don't understand why everyone lies to me and treats me like I'm stupid. All this time I thought Dad was living in some crappy apartment, working hard to get someplace where me and Mari could stay with him sometimes. He's never going to do that, is he?"

Grandad looked at me thoughtfully for a moment, "I can't speak for your dad, Ian, but I can speak for your mother. She was blindsided by these...changes...too. She's been doing her best for you and your sister in the best way she knows how."

I shook my head. "She should have been honest with us."

"Maybe, but we all make mistakes. Have you ever had trouble being honest about something that you never intended to lie about?" Grandad took a sip of his soda. His foam cup was clean and smooth, but I'd already made imprints of my thumbnail around the edges of mine. I thought about all the times I tried to tell somebody about the medallion but couldn't, even though it was never my lie in the first place.

"I guess when stuff like that happens to me, I don't wanna tell anyone about it until I've fixed the problem first, so I don't get in as much trouble," I said. "But I don't see how mom thought she was gonna fix *this*. She should have told me."

"You're right. But I believe she was trying to protect you from the hurt that she was feeling. Your mother loves you, Ian. Your dad does too. He just made some selfish choices and didn't think about how his choices would hurt the people around him."

"I feel so mad, Grandad. At both of them. At the whole world." I scraped in a new row of designs around my cup.

Grandad put his arm around me. "I can understand that. It's okay to feel angry."

Every muscle in my body was a tightly wound coil.

"But it's important that we are in control of what we do when we feel angry," Grandad said. "We don't want to make choices that hurt others the way we feel hurt, do we? It's up to you, Ian. It's up to you to choose to be better than the things that have happened to you. To be strong, and kind, and honest, even if your father hasn't been those things to you."

"It's hard to do. I don't know if I can."

"It is hard to be the kind of person God wants us to be, and you'll spend your whole life working on it. But you're not alone, Ian. You have your family. We're here to help. It's important that you don't shut out the people who love you."

I sat for a moment, thinking about that as the crowd in front of us cheered. The cow had finally laid a patty. A high school kid in a Castillo Bay Pirates T-shirt jumped up on a trailer and yelled out, "B6! Who's got ticket B6?"

"Right here! Right here!" A lady in all pink rushed forward through a mix of applauding and groaning ticket holders to accept her hundred-dollar prize. "I knew if I cheered 'er on she'd poop on my square! I've been chanting B6 at her all day!" The woman rushed through the pen and hugged the big cow before snatching her hundred-dollar bill and waving it in the air.

Grandad chuckled. "Well, I guess ol' Teriyaki came

through for somebody, didn't she?"

We both wrinkled our noses at the smell.

"Who has to clean that up?" I asked, and we both laughed. "Grandad, you started to tell me a story the other night. A story about the ship that sank with all the treasure on it. And stories about all of those ghosts…"

"Oh man, I hope I didn't scare you. Your *abuela* lit into me pretty good for spooking you with those stories."

"No, no. You didn't scare me. But I wonder…I wonder if you could tell me the rest. What happened to the people who were rescued from Captain Larsen's ship?"

****

Mom wasn't there when I went to get Maribel from the cookie tent. I was glad. I didn't know what to say to her.

"Come on," I said to Mari. "We've gotta get back to the keeper's house."

"We can't leave Mom," Mari signed. "She's so upset, Ian. Crying and crying. She just went to the bathroom to clean up. I don't want her to feel alone."

"Mom's a grown-up, Mari. She'll be fine."

Only half convinced, Mari left the tent after making me promise to text Mom.

—*I'm taking Mari to walk around.*— I pushed send.

—*I'm sorry that I*— I deleted it.

—*You should have told us the truth*— I deleted it.

—*I know it isn't your fault, but*— I deleted it.

I watched the dots dance across the screen as Mom decided what to text too.

—*Okay. Be safe.*— she responded.

—*Okay.*—

More dots. —*I love you.*—

I tried a few more responses but deleted them all and tucked my phone in my pocket without saying anything else. What was there to say?

"Let's go," I signed to Maribel.

"I didn't really have time to look at the journal very much, because I was trying to cheer Mom up. But I think First Mate Javenson figured something out about the medallion. About the way that it makes you stay a ghost."

"I learned something," I responded. "Grandad said that Captain Larsen's crew all drowned. Even the keeper who went to rescue them died."

"Do you think it was Malachi who rescued them?"

"Or didn't rescue them."

"So Malachi has been lying?" she asked.

"Well…" I looked toward the lighthouse tower in the distance, where Malachi had watched me the night before. "He definitely hasn't been telling the whole truth."

Chapter 17

Ghosts in Castillo Bay

The wind was picking up, and it swirled the sand around our feet as we crossed from the grassy festival grounds to the area in between that wasn't quite grass, wasn't quite beach.

A pair of fishermen in overalls and baseball caps paced briskly past us.

"I'm tellin' you, Poseidon's angry. I ain't never seen the sea like this," one said, scooping tobacco from a tin into his bottom lip. "One minute it's fine, and the next it's like to pull the boat right under. Somebody better tell the sea god they're sorry and make it right."

"I don't know about Poseidon nor none of that, but it's no good to be out on the water when the weather acts up as it's doin' tonight," the second agreed.

"At least there's the festival."

"Have your fun." The second fisherman snatched the tobacco tin from the first and tucked it in his back pocket. "Don't stay out too late though. Gonna head out all the earlier in the mornin' to make up for today's lost time."

"If it don't hurricane or worse on us." The first fisherman turned back to the shore and shuddered.

"Pshh. Ain't no hurricane in the forecast, you superstitious fool. It's just another storm."

"A weird storm to be sure."

The two mumbled off toward the festival where the sky looked a little brighter above the lanterns and lasers of the booths and games of the Castillo Bay Lighthouse Festival.

We pressed forward in the other direction where the lighthouse before us now looked decayed on the outside, as I knew it was on the inside. Ten-foot waves assaulted the rocky shore, slamming into the tower. Was it my imagination or had a long stair-step crack that wasn't there before formed in the bricks? The seagulls flew in circles about it, like they were vultures over something dead.

Three ghostly sailors emerged from the tall waves. One dragged a long chain behind him. The others carried pistols and daggers. Even from where I stood, I could see that each step they took toward the sand was in rhythm with their haunted shanty.

Golden, stolen, dripping with blood
Bones and truth buried deep in the mud

But this time, their trudging steps didn't stop at the shore. One foot after another, they crept up along the beach on dry land.

Maribel clutched my arm, gasping.

"I thought they couldn't come on land!" She whispered.

"Stanley said they couldn't!"

The terrifying trio continued their haunted march across the pier. The first raised his arm, chain swinging from it like a windmill. He slammed the chain on the ground. *Clink, clink, clink. Crash.* Raised it and slammed it again, striking sparks on the concrete. *Clink, clink, clink. Crash.* Behind them the other two stomped. Slow

138

and steady. Right toward the shops across the street.

"Oh no! They're headed to Captain's Cones!" Mari cried.

She was right. The three sailors stalked right up to the glossy colorful window of our favorite ice cream place. Ghostly shadows hovering over the glass illustrated with an eye-patch wearing parrot holding an ice cream cone in his wing. Big colorful words that read *X marks the spot! Sweet treasure in a carrr-amel coated cone!* Mom always made sure to read the sign in her best pirate voice when we went there. She would really dig into the *arrr* and tickle us in the ribs. We would roll our eyes at her and call her cheesy, but really, I always loved her silly pirate voice.

To my horror, the first ghost raised his pistol and shot right through the x on the window. Then, the chain-wielding ghost slung his arm around once more. *Clink, clink, clink. Shatter.* The painted glass busted under the rusted links of the spinning metal weapon. The ghost whipped his chain against the glass again and again until nothing remained but a hollow jagged hole where the dessert eating pirate parrot used to be.

The other two ghosts pulled wooden boards from the door frame and threw them into the street. They marched through the shards to the next building.

"Why are they doing this?" Mari asked.

"Malachi said they would cause us a world of trouble. I guess this is it."

I looked back to the lighthouse, planted bravely against the storm that tried to shake it. The sky was growing darker, but the light wasn't shining yet. Without the bright beacon at the top, it looked ominous. Like a tall gravestone, or the minute hand of a broken clock stalled at midnight. "They're going to keep causing this senseless destruction until we stop them."

"But how do *we* stop them? What can we do?"

"I don't know, but we can't let them get to town. Look what they did to Captain's Cones. Look what the storm is doing to the lighthouse. We've got to get back to the keeper's house, find Miss Jones, and tell her what we know. She will know what to do. We've got to find Malachi together."

"But Ian, Malachi is a—"

"A ghost. I know. But we've got to find him and convince him to help us break this curse."

Mari shuddered and took a step back. For a moment, I thought she would turn and run back to Mom the way Marcos and JC ran back to the football game. She looked up at the sky. Past me to the ghost sailors wreaking havoc on a family-owned laundromat three doors from the ice cream shop. Back at me. Mari took a step forward and grabbed my hand.

"To the lighthouse, then?"

I nodded, and I couldn't help smiling at my brave little sister. Shaking in the wind, but strong against it. Like the tower in the storm.

"To the lighthouse," I said. "Together."

So, we pushed forward into the scary mess, pretending that we were shivering from the storm and not because we were afraid of what came with it.

We saw Miss Ortiz before we made it all the way to the front of the museum. Maribel nudged me and pointed toward the keeper's house, where she was arguing with someone through the window.

The two of us ducked behind a tree to watch her. She threw up her hands and disappeared from the window frame. A moment later she stormed out of the keeper's house door.

We shuffled around the tree trunk to keep from being seen.

She tapped at her earbuds and answered a phone call.

"*Soy Camila,*" she said in a professional voice.

"She's got something in her pocket," Mari signed. I looked to where Miss Ortiz was patting the pocket of her blazer.

"I told you not to bother me until it was done." Her professional, happy voice had been replaced by something low and impatient. "I'm doing the best I can, but we've encountered some…*problemas pequeñas.*"

Miss Ortiz seemed to listen to the person on the other end of the call with growing irritation. She started shaking her head in disagreement with what they were saying, her amber hair shining with streaks of gold in the sunlight. "No, do not send them. I need more time." She rolled her eyes, listening to the person speaking as she looked around her anxiously. "Okay. Okay. *Tengo que ir,*" she said. "*Adios.*"

Miss Ortiz tapped at her ear without waiting for a reply and briskly walked to a navy rental car in the parking lot. Her tires kicked up gravel and dust as the little car disappeared down the street.

Slam. Mayor Juarez stood just outside the door of the keeper's house adjusting his tie. He turned to look back at the storm behind him and then checked his cell phone, typing out a message with furious fingers. He threw the phone back into his suit coat pocket. The mayor tugged down on the edges of his coat, took a deep breath, licked his hand to slick back his shiny black hair, and marched toward the festival grounds in a huff. We waited until he was out of sight before leaving our spot behind the tree.

"What was that about?" Mari signed.

I shook my head and shrugged my shoulders. The sooner we were done with all this, the better.

When Maribel and I arrived inside the museum, we nearly ran straight into the lighthouse keeper we were looking for.

"Miss Jones! The storm is getting bigger!"

"The ghost pirates are wrecking the town!"

"They busted up Captain's Cones—"

We talked over each other trying to tell her what we'd seen. What we'd learned.

"Kids, you're back." Her gaze darted around in a panic. "Ghosts on shore? Wrecking the town?"

"Yes, we need to get the medallion and Malachi! I think he caused the curse, and—"

"Well, that's going to be a problem," she said, running her hand through her braids.

"What do you mean?" I asked. "What's wrong?"

Miss Jones had a hurricane of her own brewing behind her frantic eyes. "The medallion is gone."

Chapter 18

Missing Again

"What do you mean the medallion is gone?" I asked, the panic in my voice rising like the tide.

"I gave a tour at two and took care of a few other things around the museum, and when I went to retrieve the medallion from my locked drawer, it was gone!"

"How could that happen?" Maribel asked.

"I don't know. I don't know." Miss Jones paced the wooden floorboards between the ship bottles and the photographs. "I've got to find my great-grandfather. He'll know what to do."

Maribel and I exchanged looks. "Miss Jones, when was the last time you saw Miss Ortiz?" I asked.

"She has been here for most of the day, working in my office." Miss Jones narrowed her eyes at us. "Why do you ask?"

We described what we'd seen to Miss Jones.

"I can't understand why she would take the medallion. I'm going to *give* it to her. We've been working on documenting the artifacts and a press release regarding the treasure. We'll have a few legal hoops to jump through, and we'll need approval from some of the donors, the lighthouse society, and possibly the mayor, but—"

"Could Mayor Juarez have taken it?" I asked.

Miss Jones pressed her mouth into a thin line. "I'm sure he isn't pleased to hear we will give away the keeper's house claim to fame if that was what they were discussing. But I can't imagine how he would know where it was to take it."

"It's got to be one of the people who were in the room when Miss Jones locked it up," Maribel said. "No one else would know where to look for it. No one knows you returned it, Ian. Everyone believes it is still missing."

I settled on my back foot. "I'm not ruling out Mayor Juarez. So that makes him, Miss Jones, Miss Ortiz, Stanley, and Malachi all suspects."

"Me?" Miss Jones's hand flew to her chest. "What about you two then?"

"We wouldn't take it!"

"You've already taken it once," she reminded me.

"Well…" I didn't know how to respond. "We didn't take it this time, Miss Jones. We've been with our family since we left you before your tour, nowhere near the lighthouse or the keeper's house."

Miss Jones studied us for a moment before relaxing her shoulders. "I'd have a hard time believing you would take it…again. I know that I didn't take it, nor would my great-grandfather. I guess that leaves Camila and…"

"Malachi," we all said together.

"Where exactly is Malachi?" I asked.

****

We found him on the shore, ankle-deep in the water, staring out at the churning ocean. The sky was growing darker, and anticipation weighed heavy on me like the purple clouds that gathered above us. When Malachi turned around, it was clear that he felt it too. His face was drawn down by the corners of his lips, and his bloodshot eyes were filled with worry.

"They're coming," he said. "The rest of them. They won't stop until they've burned the whole town to the ground."

Just past him, the ghost pirates rose from the murky water, their chant floating out over the ocean toward us along with the clinking of chains as their arms swelled up out of the waves.

Golden, stolen, dripping with blood
Bones and truth buried deep in the mud

"Malachi," I yelled over the wind and the water and the chanting. "What happened? What really happened when the ship went down?"

He squeezed his eyes shut and shook his head violently. "No. I'm sorry, kid, but I just can't…"

Golden, stolen, heavy with strife
Lies that claim each sailor's life

"If they come for me…Let them come." He took a step toward the tide.

"But they aren't just coming for you! They are coming for everyone!" I thought of my mother, sitting in her bakery booth all alone. No idea that an army of angry ghost sailors was on their way to tear everything down. Grandad and Abuela, smiling and laughing in the preservation society fundraising tent. My dad, probably playing some carnival game and Ashlee, probably hugging some big stuffed bear. Oblivious. Even stupid Marcos and JC. *Everyone is in danger, and it is all my fault.*

I spoke more gently. "I know it's hard, but you've got to tell the truth, Malachi. You've been carrying this lie too long. You don't have to bear it by yourself anymore. You're Malachi Javenson, aren't you? The first mate? What happened the day your ship sank?"

When he looked at us this time, there were tears in his eyes. "The day my captain, my crew—my friends all drowned, you mean?"

I nodded and looked at Mari, signing quickly to catch her up. There was no way she could hear anything over the swell of the storm above us. All around us.

"I never meant for any of this to happen," Malachi bellowed. "When we went with Larsen, we believed it was an archaeological expedition. But when we arrived, we learned it were no such thing. It was a slaughter. We killed and we stole and we set sail back home. Larsen threatened us that we were never to tell what really happened. I reckon I as much agreed, though I never signed up to be a pirate."

I signed the story to Mari as he spoke.

"Then he changed. Larsen. He was a good man before, but something about the medallion changed him, though I didn't know what it was. The crew wanted mutiny, but I convinced 'em to let me talk to him first. It was a full moon night, clouds threatening a storm just like this one. I went to discuss it with him calmly, like men. But Larsen wasn't in his cabin, and he wasn't in the mood for discussions. I found him out on the deck by a lifeboat, loadin' up the treasure. I guess his plan was to beat us to shore and claim the gold for himself. I tried to talk to him, but he was outta his mind with greed and rage. He pulled out his pistol and aimed it right at my forehead, cocked it. Told me to step away forever or return home never."

Golden, stolen, dripping with blood
Bones and truth buried deep in the mud
For ears that hear, the finder's fee

Is a sailor's life for the truth set free

"The clouds parted just about that time, and the light of the moon hit that thing around his neck. It was as quick as that. The waters began to change. The storm shook the skies, pouring down rain and sending down a fierce wind. Bones rose up from the deep, pulling at our ship until it darn near ripped it in two. I told Larsen to throw the medallion into the water, let the sea have it, and save his crew. But he couldn't let go of it. I went after him, tackling him across the bow and nabbing it from him so I could throw it in myself. But when it was my turn to cast it into the water, I couldn't do it."

"Why?" Maribel shouted.

"I don't know. To this day I don't know. It changed me somehow. Larsen's burden was my burden. I couldn't hear the cries of the men, couldn't think of anything but the medallion. Then I saw a boat in the distance. A rescue boat. I held up the medallion and shouted, 'Save me first and you can have this' to the rower. I showed the keeper the boat Larsen had loaded with treasure when he came for me. We loaded it onto his rescue boat instead of the men that screamed at us to save them from the choppy waters."

"You just left them there?" Horror shook my voice.

"It was wrong. It was horrible, I know. I can't explain it. I've lived tortured with it all these years." He turned back toward the dark ocean. "It's why I'm ready to let them take me. To face my punishment."

"You don't have to face punishment; we can help you. You and all of the innocent people who'll be hurt by the angry ghosts if we don't stop them. Just give us the medallion," Miss Jones shouted over the howl of the wind.

Malachi turned to face us, confusion pulling his eyebrows together. "Give you the medallion? Don't you have it?"

"No! The medallion is gone. We thought you'd taken it."

Malachi held out empty hands. "I've got no use for that cursed necklace."

"If he doesn't have it, who does?" Maribel signed.

It could be anyone. Names and ideas hammered against my skull like the rain that pelted my face and my shoulders. I thought of the little ship in the glass bottle. The tiny boat that fought against the storm. The photos from the displays along the wall.

"Who was the keeper, the lighthouse keeper who rescued you that night?" I asked him.

Another tall wave crushed against the shore. Seagulls squawked above us, fighting through the rain to rest on the railing. We all turned toward the looming shadow of the dark lighthouse.

"That'd be Jeremiah Stanley Jones," Malachi said gravely. "He's got more to lose than I do, though. Maybe he isn't as ready to face the truth as I am."

Maribel's mouth fell open. She turned to me and signed, "JSJ."

JSJ. Jeremiah Stanley Jones. The initials in the journal. The initials in the tower.

Miss Jones held her hair down against the wind that stung us with salt as she shouted over the waves. "Let's go find my great-grandfather."

Chapter 19

JSJ

I knew exactly where to find Stanley. As the four of us wound up the crumbling stairs and approached the narrow black ladder that led to the lamp room, the pull of the medallion grew stronger. Each wave threatened to take down the whole tower. Brick-mortar dust danced before us with every step we took. I coughed and waved to clear the air.

The storm was stronger than ever. I took a step back, afraid of the decrepit old lighthouse. Afraid of the pirate ghosts. Afraid of the power this medallion had over me. *I'm not strong enough for this,* I thought.

I worked my way backward, down the wobbling metal ladder with one hand scraping across the damp brick wall to brace myself.

"Come on." Maribel placed her hand on my arm. Not cold and clammy like the wall, but warm and strong. "The only way out of this is up."

I shook my head. "You don't understand," I signed. "I can't do this. I'm not strong enough to save a whole town from a crew of ghosts. We should just let the adults fix it."

"The adults got us into this mess," she answered. "We can't count on them to fix it without us."

I laughed. "Mari, I'm the one who got us into this

mess. The moment I touched that medallion. The moment I decided to lie about it. Everything just got so out of hand. None of this would have happened if I had just told Mrs. Rodriguez what happened. Or asked Mom for help. How am I going to make everything better now when I wasn't even strong enough to just return it in the first place?"

"You don't have to worry about what you should have done or whether or not you can do this," Maribel signed back. "All that matters is what we do now. You're not alone. We will figure it out together. But we have to try."

She took my hand in hers. We both took a deep breath. And we kept climbing.

We found Stanley at the top, in the lantern room. Something wasn't right about the space. It was hard to tell if it was dusk or night. Dark clouds cast shadows through the glass to the floor below, obscured through one of the sections of glass that had a crack across it, long and thin and splintering out like a spiderweb. I checked my phone. It was almost eight o'clock. Three missed text messages from my mom hovered on my notifications screen. Bright green. I tucked my phone back in my pocket without checking them.

Stanley sat with his back to us, hunched over a scattered mess of sketches and journals basking in a red glow. He struck at a match to light a lantern, but it flickered out. He pulled out another match and tried again. It sparked and disappeared just as quickly.

His muttering echoed off the glass walls. "I don't understand. It's never gone out before. It's never gone out…"

A whooshing boom of thunder rattled the room and

shook the panes around us. Pulling courage from somewhere in my belly, I asked, "What's never gone out, Mr. Jones?"

"Where is the red light coming from?" Maribel signed.

Sharply, Stanley turned to face us. His eyes were frantic, face uplit by the crimson glow of the medallion he wore around his neck, surging with power.

"The light," he said. "The beacon."

We all looked toward the center of the room to the Fresnel lens, and it settled on me why the room felt so odd under the growing grey clouds. The lamp in the lighthouse wasn't lit. The light had gone out.

I remembered reading about the Fresnel lens in class. How complicated it was. *If the lighthouse keeper can't get the light to work, what am I supposed to do?*

"Grampa, we can help with the light," Miss Jones said gently. "But why did you take the medallion?"

"Why? Because I need it! We need it. I can't let Miss Ortiz take it back to Colombia, Desiree. We've got to get the light back on and put this medallion back where it belongs. Safe. In our museum."

Miss Jones's forehead furrowed as she watched her great-grandfather squeeze the medallion tightly in one hand and clutch at his hair with the other.

"We can't put it back where it was now that we know it isn't ours to keep," she said softly.

Stanley let out a scream that shook the room along with the thunder. "It is ours. We're keepers. We keep the light on. We keep the medallion safe. We keep—"

"Oh, darn it all, Stanley, will you stop trying to protect that blasted bauble and face facts! We can't go on like this anymore!" Malachi growled. "They're coming for you for the same reason they want me. And now it's more than us they'll be punishing. It's all of Castillo Bay they'll drag down with them. All because you chose that hunk of gold around your neck over the lives of all those drowning men that night, a hundred years ago. Just like I did."

Sorrow flooded Stanley's face. He clutched the medallion tighter.

A hundred years ago?

"We said we hoped they'd find the shore. But we knew they never would. We knew we were cursing them to the depths of the ocean, and we took the treasure with us for comfort. That was before we saw that little boat over the next crest. The one coming out to help us."

Stanley squeezed his eyes shut and rocked back and forth. "No, no, no."

"That treasure wasn't worth a plug nickel to us in the end, though, was it? Death took us anyway when our rickety old boat, all weighed down with gold and nonsense, hit that rocky shore. You know what else the storm took that night? Took that little boat. Took that little boat and the people in it. That woman and her son."

"No!"

"The medallion isn't a gift, Stanley. It's a curse."

"No!"

"What is he talking about, Grampa?"

"We have to get the light on! We can't let anyone take the medallion!" Stanley was yelling now. Reaching out.

"Grampa?" Miss Jones asked. "Let's come down from here. We can discuss all this in my office or—"

"You're not bothered at all that your great-grandfather is over a hundred years old? You're not surprised that he let all those men drown or that he has cursed ghost pirates coming after him?"

Miss Jones gathered Stanley's scattered papers while he sobbed into his hands. "I've always known my great-grandfather was involved with the treasure somehow, and that he's had an extraordinarily long life. But my job isn't to be bothered right now by his story, or to be mad that he hasn't told me all of it before. Right now, it's just my job to deal with this. To help him if I can. To help all of us."

I knelt to help her with the papers. "Your great-granddaughter is right. Let's get down from here, Mr. Jones."

Stanley shuddered, clutching the medallion and crying. "I have to light the lamp. I have to get the light back on. I have to—"

Maribel placed a hand on Stanley's shoulder. "You don't have to do anything alone, Mr. Jones. We can all do it together."

Malachi placed a hand on his other shoulder. "I got us into this mess. I won't leave you alone to get out of it. I'm sure we can reverse this blasted curse. We'll do it together."

Stanley dropped the medallion and let it hang around his neck again. Emerald eyes glowed red. I remembered the moment they'd changed. The way the snake symbol had slithered all around the circle to awaken the necklace.

"Wait," I said. "I have an idea. Can you find the journal page with the symbol names?"

Miss Jones shuffled through the pages. "This one?"

"Yes. Maribel and I, we read the symbol names from the medallion and that made the eyes glow. I wonder if…"

"You can read them in reverse." Miss Jones nodded.

"Reverse the curse," Malachi muttered.

"It's worth a shot." Miss Jones flipped through the stack of papers in her hands.

Maribel helped Miss Jones find the page, and all of us looked to Stanley for the medallion.

"I'm sorry, Desiree." His lips quivered. "It's my job to protect you. To protect the lighthouse. To keep the light on. If I hand you this medallion, all might be lost. Everything might crumble."

"We're already in a heck of a mess with the whole crew crawled up from Davy Jones to drag us back with 'em, Stanley. Look up." Malachi flung a hand toward the toward the dark center of the room. "The light's already out. Half the town is wrecked. It can't get much worse than this. What say we trust the kids and let them help us bear this burden, eh?"

With trembling fingers, Stanley pulled off the necklace and placed it in Maribel's little waiting hand.

"Okay, Ian." She pointed to the last symbol.

I found it in the journal. "*Ubchihica*. Paint the shining moon."

She pointed to the next symbol.

"*Aca*. Resolved. Then *Cuhupqua*. Covered ears? *Muyhica*. Covered eyes? *Mica*. Darkness."

We all stared at the medallion; the green emeralds glowed red, buzzing with dark energy as intensely as before.

"Blast it all." Malachi crossed his arms.

"Paint the shining moon to resolve covered ears and covered eyes in the darkness…" Miss Jones ran a thumb over the symbols on the page. "Ian, try reading the words in order again without their translations. A little louder."

Maribel held the page closer, and I tried again.

"*Ubchihica, aca, cuhupqua, muyhica, mica.*"

The velvety silence of the lantern room rested on us like a dark blanket. All eyes were on the medallion, watching it radiate red with bated breath.

I was all out of ideas. *What do we do now?*

Then it happened. The snake symbol turned and wound its way back across the outside of the golden circle. When it locked in place, the emerald eyes shone brightly and flickered out, leaving us in complete darkness. The once charged and buzzing gold face sat cold and motionless in my hands.

Thunder rumbled, and a bright bolt of lightning plunged out of the clouds, through the glass, and directly into the center of the lens in the lantern room. I held my forearm up against the fierce light, then reached for Maribel as she stumbled backward.

"It's on!" Stanley shouted. "The beacon! It's shining again!"

I lowered my arm to the rotating beams of the Fresnel lens, watching them wash the shadows from each face in the room as they rotated past.

"We did it!" Maribel shouted. "We reversed the curse!"

"Well, I'll be a monkey's uncle." Malachi smacked Stanley on the back. "How about that?"

"Great job, kids." Miss Jones smiled.

Maribel and I beamed, basking in the glow of success and the spinning light from the beacon. The lighthouse was working again. *Everything is going to be okay.*

"All right, let's go put this back on display

downstairs." Stanley clapped his hands and reached for the medallion. Over his shoulder, another shot of lightning cracked across the violet sky, illuminating the shore below, and sending a bolt of terror through me, too.

A whole ghost pirate crew gathered on the shore below. Muddy boots squarely planted on dry land. Teeth bared. Weapons raised toward the rotating light of the lighthouse. Everyone in the lantern room followed my gaze.

My eyes stung with tears. "I don't understand. We reversed the curse. Why are the pirates still here?"

Their bone-chilling chant drifted up through the cracked glass.

Golden, stolen, dripping with blood
Treasure and truth buried deep in the mud
Till then the sea will hide our bones
Dark in the depths of the Davy Jones

"Ignore them," Stanley moaned. "We need to put the necklace back on display."

"Ignore them? What are they saying?" Maribel signed.

"They sing a little song. A creepy sea shanty. The pirate ghosts."

"What are they saying?"

I signed the song the best I could.

"Treasure and truth buried deep in the mud…" Maribel mulled it over. "Ian, whose bones are buried in the mud? From that legend you talked about?"

"Well, Tena's. He got so mad that Fura lied to him that he killed everybody, and then he died too."

"Covered eyes. Covered ears. Truth buried…He couldn't hear her apologize, right?"

I nodded. "That's right."

Maribel turned to Stanley and Malachi. "I think you need to apologize to the ghost pirates. Malachi, you already feel bad. You should tell them."

"Apologize? Why does it matter?" Malachi wailed. "They already know what happened. They were there!"

Their muted chant drifted up through the cracked window.

"No, I think she's right," I said. "It matters. It matters that you feel sorry. You should tell them."

"You should too, Grampa," Miss Jones said. "I love you. I'm not judging you. But you could've tried harder to save them."

"I could have," he said. "But it's too late for them. Now I'm just trying to protect you. It isn't safe to go down there and talk to them. We've got to find another way. We could look at the journals again. Put the necklace back where it belongs—"

"It belongs with Miss Ortiz, Grampa. We have to be honest too," Miss Jones said. "This treasure. All this gold. It isn't ours to keep. We've got to get it back where it belongs."

Stanley's shoulders dropped.

"Let's start with talking to the men who stole it in the first place," I said.

We stumbled down the stairway in silence, each of us contemplating the lies we needed to unravel. Each of us wondering if it would be enough to save all of us in Castillo Bay from the fury of the ghostly sailors that waited on the other side of the lighthouse door.

Chapter 20

Ghost Pirates

Dark clouds blocked the light from the moon, and everything on the shore was just a series of fuzzy purple and navy shapes when it wasn't under the fleeting light of the traveling beam from the beacon. The luminescent crew of the *Olivia,* bright white and billowing in the stormy winds, made a stark contrast. Their sea shanty beat against our ears like the series of heavy raindrops assaulting us. A growing chant.

Golden, stolen, dripping with blood
Bones and truth buried deep in the mud
Golden, stolen, heavy with strife
Lies that claim each sailor's life

"What do you want?" I shouted against the wind.

The crew stopped singing, the air growing stale with the silence. The only sound was the *dip-a-dap splash* of the rain on the rising tide. A gust of wind forced a strong blow against us and the lighthouse tower behind us, shattering the broken windowpane with a *swoosh crack!*

Maribel tucked into me, burying her tiny body between my arm and my back.

Captain Larsen bellowed out a deep gravelly cackle that rattled my ribs against my spine. Or maybe that was Maribel shaking in fear.

"What do we want?"

The crew behind him lifted ghostly hands, pointing floating fingers at me. No, behind me. I turned around to see Stanley, planted in the sand with both hands gripping the medallion.

"We gave our lives for that trinket. We want it back."

"It was never yours to die for." Malachi stomped across the shore toward the crew. "Never mine to die for either. What we did—what we did to those people at Lake Guatavita. It was wrong, Captain. We were wrong. What you did to this town. What you're plannin' to do to these people in Castillo Bay. It's all wrong."

Captain Larsen clenched his fists and thrust his elbows out. "Nothin' as wrong as betraying your captain, you yellow-bellied old fool! Who are you to stand there lecturing me on what's right. After you killed and plundered right alongside us, then left your captain and your crew to drown while you sailed away with everything we fought for!"

"I was wrong to do that too. Blinded by the treasure as you were. But I'm not now. I'm here to accept my fate. Drag me down to the depths with you if that'll appease you. Let me haunt the shores with you for all eternity. But leave these people alone. I'm sorry."

Captain Larsen dropped his arms, shocked. Behind him, the ghost crew lowered their hands. "That's fine, and all. But we'll still be needing that treasure you've got around your neck there. We may not be able to come ashore with the light back on, but we can drag the lady and the little boy down to the depths with us if need be."

"No!" Stanley screamed.

"What is he talking about, Grampa?"

Ba-boom! Thunder shook the sky, and seconds later

another flash of lightning illuminated the shore.

A slam and swinging creak echoed out from the keeper's house behind us. A woman, tall and beautiful like Miss Jones, strode across the sand toward Stanley. She held the hand of a little boy. A boy about Maribel's age. A red rose in her hair glimmered beneath flashes of purple light.

"Sarah, please! Go back inside! It isn't safe out here," Stanley hollered.

The woman floated gracefully forward. She placed a hand on Miss Jones's cheek as she passed.

"Who are you?" Miss Jones asked in a whisper.

"I'm your great-grandmother," she said. "My name is Sarah Jones."

I looked at the boy again. He was holding a little toy boat like the ones from the display case. It was the boy from the picture of the keeper's family.

"Thomas?" I asked.

"Hi," the little boy said. "How does he know my name, Dad?"

"Dad?" Miss Jones turned to her great-grandfather.

The child ran to embrace Stanley, and the woman walked to his side to take his hand.

Stanley kissed the boy on the head, and when he looked up, there were tears streaming down his face. "This is my family," he said. "My wife. My son."

"But how—"

"They died in the storm," Malachi said. "Coming out on a little boat to help us."

"Died?" Maribel asked.

"The medallion keeps the ghosts alive," Miss Jones said. "I understand."

"I thought if I could just put it back, everything

would go back to the way it was. When we could still be a family, and I could still keep those pirates at bay."

"Darling." Sarah tipped her husband's chin up with a gentle finger. "We've been enjoying this fantasy for far too long. Don't you think it's time? Time to return it to where it came from. Time for us to pass on."

"No!" Larsen yelled. "It isn't your choice to make. That treasure belongs to me!"

A member of the crew stepped forward. "It doesn't belong to us, captain. If that's the meaning of this curse, then I don't want no part in it neither. I didn't want no part in hurting those people."

"First Mate Javenson is right," another said. "He was always right. We shouldn't have done it. I'm sorry."

Murmurs of agreement went up from the crew. But Jeremiah and Sarah looked at each other for a long while. As if they were memorizing the lines of one another's faces, even though they'd had a hundred years to learn them. As if on cue they both looked down to Thomas.

"We'll still be together, won't we?" Thomas asked.

"Of course," Sarah said. "Family never stops being family. No matter what it looks like. No matter where they go."

Maribel squeezed my hand.

"I'm ready, Dad," Thomas said.

Stanley turned to Miss Jones. He pulled the medallion from his neck and extended his hand toward her. "I was afraid to let you send everything back to Colombia. I was afraid of losing my family. Worried the ghosts would storm these shores and hurt us all. I see now that I was wrong. A little cowardly, maybe. But I only ever lied to you because I was trying to protect my family. Protect you. Protect you from all of the terrible sadness out in the world. Protect you from the shameful choices I'd made."

"Grampa, I—"

"No, no." Stanley placed the medallion face up in his great-granddaughter's hands. "I can see that you don't need me to bear this burden for you anymore. Your heart is pure and strong. I'm so proud of you. I know you'll always do the right thing. Better than your old great-grandfather, anyhow."

Miss Jones's eyes glistened with tears. "I understand, Grampa. I love you."

"I love you too, Desiree. You know the truth now. I hope you don't judge me too much."

Stanley walked farther down the beach, hand in hand with Sarah and Thomas until he stood shoulder to shoulder with Malachi.

"It's an awful sentence, living with guilt for eternity. I'm ready to accept my fate and pass on."

Captain Larsen laughed again. "Pass on? There's no passing on for any of us. You're doomed by that Colombian gold the same as the rest of us. Cursed."

Above us, the clouds parted to let in one thin beam from the moon above them. It trickled down like water across jagged rocks, bouncing first off dense curls of clouds, then the black cap of the lighthouse, traveling the stairsteps of cracked bricks along the tower, washing down the shore, until finally, it danced along Miss Jones's arm and reflected off the two emerald stones in the center of the medallion in her palm. The moonbeam grew wider, pushing the clouds back.

"I can see it. The way home." Malachi began to shimmer, becoming transparent. "You did it, kids. I knew you could. Thank you." A moment later, there was nothing but air where he'd stood. Air and dancing specks of purple light.

"This is it," Stanley said, squeezing the hands of his family beside him. "Are you ready?"

"We're ready," Sarah answered, smiling.

"Keep the light on, Desiree," Stanley shouted.

Desiree nodded. "I will," she whispered.

Just as Malachi had disappeared, so did Stanley, Sarah, and Thomas.

Members of the crew turned to one another, examining their shimmering arms and legs as they, too, faded into the moonlight.

Up from the ocean, the football team appeared. Fabric jerseys and leather helmets. The team cheered and cried as they, too, ran toward the moonbeam until they became nothing but dust dancing in the air.

With every ghost gone, the moon shone a little brighter. The clouds seemed to shrink and disappear. The storm was gone.

"Never," Larsen growled. "I'll never trade in treasure for fairy dust. There's nothing to be sorry for. That trinket belongs to me!"

"The only thing that belongs to you is an eternity of doubt and despair. If you like gold so much, go back to the bottom of the ocean. There's plenty of it down there." Desiree tucked the medallion into her pocket. "Come on, kids. It's time to find Miss Ortiz."

I looked over my shoulder as we walked back up to the keeper's house.

Captain Larsen stood with his hands balled into fists of stubborn rage at the shore, unable to step onto the sand, figures glimmering and fading all around him.

Chapter 21

Fireworks

Mom was wrestling with the pop-up tent when we found her. Popping in metal notches at each corner and shimmying the canvas down section by section. She paused, pulled her phone from the back pocket of her jeans, and stared at it, then put it back and worked at the metal accordion frame.

"Let me help you," I said, joining her at one corner.

Mom looked up, surprised, and a watery-eyed smile spread across her face.

"Me too," Mari added, going to another corner.

We lowered the tent and pushed it together, meeting at the center.

"Thank you," she said. "That was hard to do alone."

"It's not a job for one person."

I turned around to see Grandad and Abuela approaching with armfuls of lawn chairs. "You kiddos ready to set up for the fireworks?"

"Absolutely!" Mari ran to Grandad to take a chair from his arms.

"I'm going to help Mom pack this stuff up first," I said.

Grandad winked at me. "Sounds like a plan. We'll set up a chair for you."

Mom and I carried boxes to the Castillo Bay Cookie

Palace delivery van. I marveled at the sky above us, clear and calm. The threatening storm had hovered so long it had seemed to become normal.

Mom pulled open the back doors of the van.

"Ian," Mom started. "About your father."

"I don't want to talk about Dad," I said, lifting a cardboard box into the back of the van. "He made his choices. I'll figure things out with him."

Mom loaded in the last box, then closed the doors. She let out a deep sigh and rested on the edge of the tailgate. "I'm sorry that all of this hurt you, son. I tried so hard to protect you from all of it."

"I know," I said, sitting beside her.

Mom reached her arm around me, and I let her pull me in.

Music rattled out of speakers posted around the festival grounds and the first set of fireworks shot off.

"I'm doing the best I can," Mom said as we stared up at the blossoms of bursting red lights in the sky. "I just want you kids to be okay."

Another set of sparks went up. Bright golden suns and glittering green jewels. I thought of the eyes from the medallion. Of all the things people said to try and save themselves.

To try and protect each other.

"We will be okay, Mom. All of us will be okay."

The shimmering lights reflected on Mom's cheeks, wet with tears. She nodded. "Are you ready to go back?"

"Yes," I said. "I'm ready."

We closed the doors and headed back to the row of lawn chairs where Grandad, Abuela, and Maribel were enjoying the show. Everyone sang along to the familiar country song that boomed out of the speakers as a new set of red fireworks marched upwards.

We passed by Miss Jones and Miss Ortiz, sitting on a blanket and drinking sodas. Mayor Juarez was wagging a finger at them, his black hair disheveled and falling over one side of his forehead. They listened patiently to his rant, sipping at their sodas and smirking at one another.

"Some show, huh?" Grandad asked as we took our chairs.

"Some show." Mom ruffled Maribel's hair and sat next to her.

I took a seat by Abuela.

"Let me see that coin again, *mijo*," she said. "I never got a good look at it."

I reached into my pocket and pulled out a handful of stuff. Two keys, the coin, and a dried rose petal. I ran my thumb over the petal, recalling Sarah and Thomas, and glanced up at Abuela. She smiled at me with gentle crinkles cradling her eyes. And I realized why I'd liked Stanley's smile so much. I handed her the coin. One of the biggest fireworks yet set off with the crescendo of the ballad, a high singing *skiii-boom* that rattled our stadium chairs. *Crack. Crackle. Crackle.* Fiery white bursts danced across the shining surface as she turned it over, examining it.

"We talked about this in our fundraising tent today," Abuela said. "I told everyone how much you enjoyed the scavenger hunt. How many kids want to visit the tower."

"That light is a big deal," I agreed.

"It is. We're all worried Mayor Juarez will ruin the integrity of all this with his fancy plans to change everything." Abuela handed the coin back to me. "But I guess, change isn't always bad."

Behind my *abuela*, the mayor stomped off. Miss Jones and Miss Ortiz giggled and tapped their plastic cups together in a cheers.

"No," I agreed. "But I think Mayor Juarez may be rethinking that whole plan, anyway."

Abuela looked after him and laughed. "That man is always worked up about something."

"Maybe we could come up with a plan together," I said, rolling the coin over my knuckles. "A plan to raise money and have people restore the lighthouse the right way. There has to be some option between letting it crumble into ruin or replacing it with something completely different."

Abuela smiled. "Did I ever tell you that you're a pretty smart cookie?"

I beamed, hoping she didn't notice me blushing under the lights from the fireworks.

A new song rang out across the festival grounds. Cheerful and upbeat. Yellow sparklers blasted in a chorus line, and a multicolored chrysanthemum burst into a shower of shooting twinkling stars.

"Oh, I love those." My mom sighed.

Behind Miss Jones and Miss Ortiz, my dad was sitting in a lawn chair with Miss Ashlee on his lap. A giant stuffed bear sat in the dirt by the chair, slumped against his shoe. Ashlee placed her cowboy hat on Dad's head and pointed up at the burning lights above us. He sported a big smile, and they both laughed and cheered. I swallowed hard. I remembered the way Miss Ortiz said that Tena's rage from being lied to caused destruction for everyone, even him. I thought of Captain Larsen, planted on the beach with balled fists and gritted teeth while everyone around him passed peacefully. He'd been ready to set everyone loose on the whole town to destroy everything, and even now his anger was holding him back. I took a deep breath and decided to let my anger go. Like bones sinking to the ocean floor. Like a metal anchor dropping. Like the little explosions of light in the sky above us.

Family never stops being family. No matter what it looks like. No matter where they go.

My dad's hand patted Miss Ashlee's thigh as she giggled and clapped. *I'm not ready to sit with them,* I thought. *But I'm not mad anymore.*

And I felt lighter. Free.

Chapter 22

Monday

"Ian, this paper is phenomenal," Mrs. Rodriguez said, handing back my report with a big red 100 sprawled across the top and a little sticker with a smiling yellow pencil giving a thumbs up. "I'm really proud of you!"

"Thank you." I tucked the paper neatly in my folder, thinking about how excited my mom would be to hang it on the fridge later.

"I love your ideas about fundraising for the lighthouse society."

"My *abuela* said she would help me get a committee together," I said. "A lot of businesses were damaged in the storm at the festival. We can get volunteers together to help them clean up and rebuild. Then we would plan to have contractors who specialize in historical landmarks take a look at the lighthouse tower so they can make it safe and fun but still preserve its history."

"That's fantastic. My uncle's laundromat was completely demolished that night. He was devastated. Let me know how I can help." Mrs. Rodriguez walked down the rows, distributing the rest of the papers.

I caught Marcos and JC groaning out of my side-eye as she handed back theirs without stickers, just a series of notes.

"See me after class, Marcos," Mrs. Rodriguez said.

"There were no sharks at the lighthouse or anywhere in the museum, and I know you plagiarized most of your paper word for word from Wikipedia. This was meant to be your original writing." She walked on.

"Whaa? But—!" Marcos slumped down in his chair and broke his pencil in half. "Bruh."

The bell rang. I gathered my things.

Marcos grabbed my arm when I tried to tuck my folder into my bag. "Ian, dude. Help me write a new paper."

"No, Marcos." I shook him off and slung my backpack over my shoulder.

"What? Why! I'm gonna fail if you don't help me!"

I glared at him. "Sounds like a *you* problem."

"Save it," JC said to Marcos. "He's just a little kiss-up these days. Teacher's pet. Gotta make Mommy proud."

"Hey, Ian," Dominic shouted from the door frame. "You got science next, right?"

I pushed past Marcos and JC, ignoring their hateful expressions and the back half of a pencil that flew past my ear. I tried not to laugh when I heard Mrs. Rodriguez shout both of their names and threaten them with lunch detention.

"You know," Dominic said as I met him in the hall. "Just because you don't play football anymore doesn't mean you have to hang out with losers who treat you like crap and get you in trouble all the time."

I shoved my hands into my pockets and kept walking. "You're right."

"I know."

I was looking down at my shoes, so I almost bumped into a guy in front of me.

"Sorry," I mumbled, stumbling backward.

"That's cool, cat," the guy said. He took a comb out of his letter jacket pocket and slicked back his hair.

"Cat..." My eyebrows pressed together.

"Come on, Frankie!" A girl with a bouncy bright ponytail ran up to take his hand. Her pink poodle skirt swayed as they skipped down the hallway. "We're gonna miss the sock hop!"

I stood frozen by the lockers.

"You okay?" Dominic asked.

The science class door was open. Students were taking their seats. There was a spot for me at the table with my friends. The ones who didn't make fun of me, prank me, or get me in trouble. Turned out my real friends didn't actually care if I played football or not. They didn't care if my parents were divorced.

"Yeah," I said, stepping toward class. "I'm okay."

Down the hallway, the guy in the letter jacket spun his girl in a circle, looked right at me, and winked.

Acknowledgments

The shaping of an author begins early. This time, I would like to start my acknowledgments by thanking my teachers. I have been fortunate to be guided and encouraged by a series of stellar educators throughout my life who helped me become the writer I always wanted to be. Special thanks to Tina Wuensche, Carolyne Wilson, Carolyn Bodystun, Connie Lee, Rachel Lehman Vega, Carletta Renfro, Arlene Stephens Spearman, Altah Swindle, Carroll Rhodes, and Kelly Kieth who taught me as a student and a teacher. All the love, time, and care you poured into me as a student gave me the courage and inspiration to take on the world in whatever way I wanted to. I think about you every time I step into a classroom to educate the next generation of students.

I have also been very blessed to be raised by a world-renowned educator who has dedicated her life to building the knowledge of others, my mom, Cathy Box. Mom, when you realized that I learned differently from others, you devoted your time and energy to figuring out what would work best for kids like me. You were the first person to believe I could be a writer. Without you, I might still be wandering around, lost in the elementary school halls distracted by anything shiny. Thank you to my dad and biggest supporter, Ray Box. Dad, you taught me the value of the library and read us books every night for as long as I can remember. Now, you read them to my children and provide them with the kind of love and grace they need to grow, which served as inspiration for Ian's grandfather in this book.

Thank you to my sisters, Kristin Goen and Nikki Tekell, my best friends, for all of your support and encouragement. The only thing better than having you as sisters is getting to enjoy the way you love on my kids as aunts.

Mason and Brady, it is an absolute joy to be your mom. I am so proud of your strength, your bravery, your kindness, cleverness, and endless curiosity. Thank you for joining me on the journey to writing this book, chapter by chapter, and line by line.

Thank you to my beta readers Hagin and Katy Gustin for your valuable feedback. You are both so impressively insightful!

I'd like to thank my students, past, present, and future. It's such a joy to watch you all grow as readers and writers. Your willingness to learn and grow inspires me to do the same.

To The Wild Rose Press and my fabulous editor, Eilidh MacKenzie. Eilidh, you improve every piece of writing that you touch. Thank you for investing your time and expertise in *The Curse of Castillo Bay Lighthouse* and for your commitment to making me and my work the best it can be.

As always, thank you to my wonderful husband, Jeremiah Denning. The entire trajectory of my life changed when I met you. You taught me what love looks like when you have a supportive partner who believes in you and helps you shoot for the stars.

Until next time.
Sarah Denning

A word about the author...

Sarah Denning is from Tahoka, TX, with a Bachelor's Degree in Art and Design from Abilene Christian University and a Master's in Literature from Wayland Baptist University. She also writes adult mystery fiction, including her recent fan-favorite Circus Train at Sunrise. She is a middle school Language Arts and Reading teacher in Texas. Sarah lives in Lubbock with her husband Jeremiah and their beautiful blended family that includes four children, Alleigh, Mason, Aubrey, and Brady.

Thank you for purchasing
this publication of The Wild Rose Press, Inc.

For questions or more information
contact us at
info@thewildrosepress.com.

The Wild Rose Press, Inc.
www.thewildrosepress.com